MW01125368

THE WALKING MAN

Other books by Constance O. Irvin

The Seasons of a Heart, 2005

THE WALKING MAN

A NOVEL

CONSTANCE O. IRVIN

iUniverse, Inc.
New York Lincoln Shanghai

The Walking Man

Copyright © 2007 by Constance O. Irvin

All rights reserved. No part of this book may be used or reproduced
by any means, graphic, electronic, or mechanical, including
photocopying, recording, taping or by any information storage
retrieval system without the written permission of the publisher
except in the case of brief quotations embodied in critical articles
and reviews.

iUniverse books may be ordered through booksellers or by contacting:

iUniverse
2021 Pine Lake Road, Suite 100
Lincoln, NE 68512
www.iuniverse.com
1-800-Authors (1-800-288-4677)

Because of the dynamic nature of the Internet, any Web addresses
or links contained in this book may have changed
since publication and may no longer be valid.

This is a work of fiction. All of the characters, names, incidents,
organizations, and dialogue in this novel are either the products of the
author's imagination or are used fictitiously.

Cover photo: Historic American Engineering Record
War Eagle Bridge, Benton County, Arkansas AR-50-2

Photographer: Louise T. Taft

ISBN: 978-0-595-43406-0 (pbk)
ISBN: 978-0-595-87730-0 (ebk)

Printed in the United States of America

To the memory of Bobby

CHAPTER 1

What greater thing is there for human souls than to feel that they are joined for life—to be with each other in silent unspeakable memories.

—George Eliot

If a person wanted to come to Taneytown, about the only way to get there is by car. Old Highway 280 runs by it not long after you cross the Cahaba River headed north toward Birmingham. My name is Margaret Green, and that's where I'm going.

A small sign reading Taneytown points left. Once you make the turn and drive over another bridge, it looks like the small village is trapped in the 1950s. Most of the stores still operate as they did then, but most of the people I remember are gone. Some died, one got murdered, one committed suicide, and some just left for cities like Birmingham or Memphis or Atlanta.

I ended up living in Michigan and finally in Florida, and over the next fifty-some years, I lost track of what had become of Taneytown. But the summer of 1950 will always be in my memory. That's why I am going back: to keep a promise made so long ago.

My family wasn't born in Alabama; we were transplants. For many families, after World War II, work was scarce, and our family was no exception. Dad was a sign painter, but his job in the small town of Carlisle, Pennsylvania, wasn't enough to "make ends meet," as Mom was fond of saying. In 1945, when I was just four years old, Dad read that Birmingham had a lot of work. After much discussion, the decision was made to go.

1

My family—Mom, Dad, my older brother Charlie, and I—packed up our belongings and went, but we didn't go to the city. Dad didn't mind working in Birmingham, but he didn't want us to live there. The dirt and grime of the steel and iron industries permeated the valley below Red Mountain, where the huge Vulcan statue stood watch over a city with air that was forever hazy with dust. It was not like the Amish cleanliness of Carlisle.

Dad looked for a place that reminded him of Pennsylvania, with its fishing streams and quiet rolling hills. That's how Taneytown became our home. Although we were first looked upon with suspicion because we were "Yankees," it didn't take our family long to fit into the easy life of the Alabama hills and to be accepted by the many friendly people who lived in and around the village.

As a kid, I loved being able to come and go, and I spent endless hours outside after school and through the summer playing in the woods and swimming in the Cahaba. Most of the time, the only thing that brought Charlie and me out of the woods was Dad's shrill whistle. When Charlie and I heard it, we knew it was time for supper.

There's an old saying that you can't go home again, and maybe that's true. A lot happened in the summer of 1950 that changed many lives—some good things, some bad. The funny thing is that I still remember my years there with fondness, maybe even a mix of joy and melancholy, but not sadness. The promise I had made so many years before brought me back, just like Dad's whistle. When I drove across the new concrete bridge to Taneytown, I stopped and tried to remember how the old iron truss bridge with the plank roadway had looked. Some memories are never lost, and I could still see the bridge, the dirt river road, and, up ahead, the village, with its scattering of one-story brick buildings.

It all came back to me: the people, the lazy days of summer, the smell of red clay, the coolness of the Cahaba River, and the calls of mockingbirds. It was a long time ago, when all of us were innocent.

CHAPTER 2

August, 1950

"Hey, Cotton, you want to follow Wallis? I just saw him leave the post office."

Cotton walked over to me, a grin spread across his tanned face, his long white hair blowing in the morning breeze. "Yeah," he said. "Maybe we'll find out what he's up to and where he goes all the time."

The game began. We'd pick up reinforcements along the way. Angel and her little sister Ida Mae, my best friend Buddy, and sometimes my older brother Charlie would join in to follow Wallis Walker, the thin, tall man with the piercing blue eyes, scraggly hair, and crooked smile. We knew his name, but most people in town just called him the Walking Man. He could walk for miles and miles.

Funny how when you're a kid, you just accept somebody that looks kind of peculiar. I mean, us older kids did, but Angel's little sister Ida never did really accept him. She'd see him and grab Angel's dress and whine, "He's a witch. He's a witch!" We just laughed and would shame the little five year-old to get her to go with us. If she didn't, then Angel couldn't go. All of us wanted Angel to go because she was so special, with her curly, coal-black hair, light green eyes, and that wonderful smile. It made me happy just to see her. She was kind to everybody. That's why we loved her. Angel.

It's not easy to have four or five kids follow a person around in a small place like Taneytown, but we did it most mornings. Wallis started at the post office. Sometimes he even got mail, although we never could imagine who would write letters to him, because we were convinced he couldn't read. We spent hours trying to figure out a way to get his mail. Of course, after we found out it was a federal offense, we dropped that idea fast. I was nine years old, and I didn't want to spend the rest of my life in jail over some dumb letter. Anyway, the fun was just in trying to follow him without him seeing us.

"You think he'll go into Sue Ann's this morning?" I asked.

Cotton twisted his mouth. "I hope not. I hate waiting around for him to come out. I don't see how anybody can spend hours drinking a cup of coffee."

He motioned for me to follow him into a passage between Lyle's Barber Shop and Deeter's General Store. We stood in the shadows, waiting for the Walking Man. Sure enough, within minutes, there he was, just like every other day. On that day, Wallis wore all black clothes and a crumpled black cowboy hat. Wow. If Ida Mae could have seen him, she would have been convinced he was a witch. I almost believed it myself.

"Damn," Cotton whispered. "He's goin' into Sue Ann's grill. Now we'll have to wait."

"I don't mind. Let's go inside Deeter's and look at the candy. I got twenty-five cents."

Cotton studied my face hard. "You foolin'? Twenty-five cents? That'll buy plenty. You must have all your money saved for your BB gun." Cotton about knocked me down getting around the edge of the brick building. I heard the door to Deeter's squeak open before I reached the sidewalk.

Deeter's was the only store I knew that was open seven days a week. Us kids were glad for that, especially in the summertime. We could go in there every day if we wanted to, and we usually did, whether we had money to spend or not.

Deeter's smelled like sugar the minute you stepped inside. The glass candy cases formed a long line from the front door towards the back. There must have been twenty feet of penny candy, three shelves tall. I looked and looked at every piece, but most times, I only ever bought the pinwheels. I loved those the best. The chocolate part was my favorite, because the white swirl was too sugary for me. Cotton would eat any and all of it if he could. Deeter's had ice cream too. It was heaven inside that store.

Deeter came from the back carrying a gun and a rag. He wiped the barrel of the pistol as his heavy body moved toward us. "Hey, you two. What are you up to today?"

"Nothin'," Cotton answered.

Deeter smiled. His rotten front teeth gave him a sinister look, but he wasn't mean to us kids at all. "Your uncle still want a good firearm?" Tobacco juice dribbled down one corner of his mouth.

Cotton turned from the candy cases. "I reckon."

"Well, tell him I got this here new Colt, and I'll make him a deal if he wants to turn in his over-and-under."

Cotton laughed. "Now, Deeter, you know Uncle Bob'll never give up that ol' shotgun. Why don't you just let up on that?"

"Well, tell him anyway. You never know. This is a mighty fine gun." He pretended to shoot a stuffed pheasant, which was hung with clear fishing line above cases of handguns, knives, and assorted hunting and fishing gear on the other side of the room. Separating the guns and the candy were shelves of canned goods, shovels, bolts of cloth, string, nails, and pots and pans. Toward the back wall stood racks of dresses, blouses, shirts, and pants. The store had just about anything anybody could ever want.

"Now, Miss Maggie," Deeter said to me. "Have you saved your money for your own BB gun?"

"Yes. Dad's going to come down with me to get it. It's still just four ninety-five, isn't it?"

"Last time I checked." He smiled. The juice dribbled.

Cotton was intent on the candy. "Can I have five pieces of licorice and five caramels?"

"You got any money?"

"Maggie does."

I fingered the dimes and nickel inside the pocket of my jeans. "I want ten swirls."

Deeter moved behind the candy cases and laid the Colt on the glass top. "Should I put it all in one bag?"

"Separate, please." I knew darn well Cotton would eat mine too if everything was in one bag.

The back door banged open and shut. Deeter frowned. "Is that you, Randal?"

"Yeah."

"You're late again," Deeter said as he counted candy into a bag.

Randal Turner walked towards the front. "I know. But I had to fix my car."

"You need to give up that piece of junk." Deeter said.

Randal twisted a hunk of his sandy hair and looked at me. I quickly turned away. He was the son of the piano player for the Baptist church. I didn't like Randal, and I didn't know why. He had never done anything to me, but I found it strange that he painted his car, a dented Crosley, about once a week. The paint would hardly be dry, and he'd be at it again. Weird colors, too: turquoise, orange, school bus yellow. Townspeople said that being in the war had made him odd, but I didn't know much about wars and what they might do to a person. I stole a look at him, and he was still looking at me with his dark, fierce eyes. I moved closer to the counter.

"Here's your candy." Deeter pushed my bag at me. Cotton was already chewing on a stick of licorice.

"Maggie, come on." Cotton sounded anxious. "We gotta go." I looked out the window and saw Wallis starting down the street.

"Here." I practically threw the money on the counter. "I'll be back, Deeter. I want my BB gun."

The screen door slammed behind me. Cotton was already twenty feet ahead, hot on Wallis's trail.

The Walking Man usually set a fast pace. Sometimes we had to run to keep him in sight, but this morning, he was in no hurry. I caught up to Cotton. "Do you think he'll go in the woods today?" I asked.

"How should I know? I don't even think he knows where he's going."

We continued at the slow pace until we ran out of town, which wasn't much of a town, just a few stores, a movie house, a gas station, the jailhouse, and bars—mostly bars. As we neared the crossroad that ran alongside the river, Cotton stopped. Wallis had turned right.

"I'm goin' to get Buddy," Cotton said. "You watch him. I'll be right back."

Cotton wheeled left and ran down the dirt road towards the small house where Buddy and his mom and two younger sisters lived. Buddy's dad wasn't much on fixing up anything, so the house was really a shack. I never liked going there because I was afraid that I might fall through the holes in the front porch. The last time I visited Buddy, a snake had crawled out from under the porch and slithered across the dirt yard. It scared the bejesus out of me. Buddy simply chopped off its head with a shovel. After that, I stayed clear.

I stood on the corner, looking after Wallis, who was disappearing down the road. I turned impatiently to look for Cotton and Buddy. There was no sign of them. When I turned back, Wallis was gone. Damn. Cotton would sure be mad at me. I started running towards the place where I had last seen the Walking Man.

Buddy yelled, "Slow down! We're comin'."

"Y'all wait. We're coming too."

I recognized Angel's voice and smiled. She was so sweet. I stopped dead in my tracks to wait. Angel appeared with Ida Mae straggling behind. The little girl giggled.

Having the bunch of us together would make following the Walking Man hard, but I didn't care. I was so happy to see Angel that nothing else mattered.

"You want a pinwheel?" I asked, as Angel neared me. This morning, she was wearing a fluffy pink-and-white dress. Around her neck, she wore a gold cross on a braided chain. It glistened in the sun. Her Mary Jane shoes were shiny, and she had a pink bow in her hair. She sure was pretty.

She smiled at me. "I'd love one," she said. "May Ida Mae have one too?"

I dug in my paper sack. Heck, Angel could have anything she wanted from me. Since Ida Mae was her sister, she could too.

"Here." I handed her the candy.

"I like caramel." Ida turned the pinwheel over in her hand.

"Ask Cotton for some. He's got five pieces."

Cotton and Buddy had caught up to us. "No, I don't. Not anymore. I ate 'em all. Where's Wallis?"

"I don't know." I shrugged. "I suppose I need to give Buddy a pinwheel."

Cotton gave me a hard look. "Yep. That's your punishment for losing sight of the Walking Man." He rolled a caramel around in his mouth as he talked.

"Well, it wouldn't have happened if you hadn't taken so long getting here," I said as I handed Buddy a pinwheel.

"It was my fault," Buddy offered. "I had a chore I was just finishin'."

I was sorry I had said anything. Buddy had to do most of the work around his house, and I knew for a fact that his dad, Alton, beat him if he didn't get his chores done when he thought they should be done. It didn't make any difference how much work there was. Buddy had to move fast or take a licking. I thought Mr. Toliver just liked an excuse for the beatings. Anyway, Buddy never said anything about them, but all us kids saw the bruises. We knew.

Buddy was the oldest in our group, almost eleven. He was strong, and in spite of the red hair on his head, he didn't have a temper. It was a good thing, because he could have whipped us all if we ever got in real serious fights. But we were friends; fights were rare.

"I don't need a pinwheel, Maggie," Buddy said. "You eat 'em. Besides, I bet Cotton has caramel left, and he's got one for me and one for Ida Mae." He handed the candy back to me.

Cotton looked sheepish. "Oh, heck, I was just kiddin', Maggie." He dug into his shirt pocket and pulled out two caramels. "Here Buddy."

Ida Mae smiled as Buddy handed one to her. She quickly stuck the caramel in her mouth. The juice from the pinwheel stained the collar on her blue cotton dress. I watched as Angel licked a finger and rubbed the goo off Ida's collar.

"So, what's the plan now?" Buddy asked.

"I think he went into the woods, down by the willow where the river bends." I tried to sound like I knew where he went, even though I didn't. Not for sure.

"Let's go, then." Cotton started off, and we all followed.

Once we got off the dirt road, we stepped as quiet as we could into the woods. It was mostly made up of tall pine, with oak trees scattered here and there. The pine needles made walking easy, except for Buddy, who seldom wore shoes. Every once in a while, he'd let out a short whoop and stop to pull a needle from his toe.

We walked for some time in silence before coming to the foot of a small, craggy mountain. A faint trail, probably made by animals that roamed in the night, went up the side. We decided to follow it. Buddy led the way, with Cotton behind him. Angel and Ida Mae struggled up the path after them, and I held the rear. I marveled at how Angel could keep up in her shoes. I had only tried on Mary Jane shoes once, but I didn't like how they looked or fit. They weren't made for Alabama clay and rocky hills. I was glad I had my sneakers on. Buddy fairly buzzed along on his bare feet. We moved at a steady pace, not knowing where we were going, but we sure were going. Even when brush began to slow us down, we kept going farther and farther up the mountain.

As much as we had played in the woods, we had never come this way before. We didn't know if Wallis was anywhere nearby, but it was an adventure. A serious game.

A deadly game.

CHAPTER 3

We walked along in silence for maybe twenty minutes. Sometimes Ida Mae would whine about being tired. Angel would whisper, "Shhhh. Just a little farther."

Cotton stopped and motioned for us to be quiet. We all tried to look ahead of him. I heard something that sounded like falling water. There was no other sound. Cotton moved on. As we leveled off near the top of the ridge, Buddy suddenly ran ahead and disappeared around a bend.

He yelled back. "Come on! It's a waterfall."

We forgot about Wallis and the need for quiet. Cotton flew to Buddy's side. Angel and Ida Mae stepped up their pace, and soon all of us stood on the ridge, looking down to another smaller ridge where a waterfall tumbled over rocks and boulders. An uprooted oak tree arched over the crest of the fall. At the bottom, a pool of clear, cool water invited us down.

True to form and with great glee, Buddy was first. He jumped right in. Of course, he didn't have to worry about shoes. The rest of us scrambled over a log and stood at the edge of the stream.

"I best not go in, y'all," Angel said. "But Ida can." She stooped to remove her sister's lace-topped socks and her Buster Brown shoes. As she waded into the water, Ida Mae squeaked with delight.

I untied my Keds and laid them carefully on the log with my socks. As I rolled up my jeans, I asked, "How come you're not going in, Angel?"

"I don't want to get my dress wet. Mama would have a hissy fit if I came home all muddy." She rolled her eyes and added, "Well, really, I just don't want to get dirty."

I loved Angel, but sometimes I didn't understand her. Heck, I wouldn't miss a chance to get all wet and have fun. The water felt good on my feet. The sandy bottom gave way to a bed of large stones and rocks. The boys had moved into the center of the pool and were splashing one another. Cotton cupped his hand and let fly a tremendous shelf of water that hit me square in the eyes.

"Dang you, Cotton! I'll get you for that." I tried my best to send sheets of spray his way, but it really didn't matter. He was totally wet. He just grinned. And then he and Buddy dove down and got behind some of the boulders that jutted out of the water. I flopped backward into the coolness. My pigtails floated like outstretched wings.

We played for some time. Silly games like retrieving stones from the deepest part. We played King of the Rock, which I always lost, and we saw who could stay under the longest, which I always won. Summer games. Kid games.

"Y'all just plumb forgot about the Walking Man, didn't ya'll?" Angel was sitting on the log, watching.

"Naw, we didn't forget," Buddy said. "We should get on with our followin'."

I moved towards shore, stubbing my toes as I went. I sat on the log next to Angel. "Dang, those rocks hurt your toes."

"Well, then. I suppose you won't do this again."

"Sure I will. I just won't wear my good Keds. I'll wear an old pair and swim in them."

Angel gave me a weird look. "You mean to say that you'd swim in your shoes?"

"Of course I would. I don't have crusty feet like Buddy."

"Maggie, you are just too much." She squeezed me tight and kissed me on the cheek. I about fell off the log. I might have loved her more than I loved Buddy. Maybe even more than Buddy loved her.

"Come on, Ida. Get out. We're goin' again." Angel held out her hand. The little girl tiptoed to shore.

By the time Angel had put Ida Mae's socks and shoes back on her, the boys were doing a balancing act on the fallen tree at the crest of the waterfall. They crossed to the other side of the stream while I helped Angel get Ida up the incline.

Angel looked across the log. "I don't think I can do this. It's a long ways down if you fall."

"Buddy," I called. "Help us. Angel and Ida Mae don't have the right shoes for this."

Buddy raced back to the log. "Heck. This ain't nothin'." He scurried across and offered Angel his hand. She stepped up, and Ida Mae followed. I waited as they inched their way to the other side. Buddy must have been tickled to hold Angel's hand for so long. I envied him. I should have helped them myself.

"Come on, Maggie." Buddy grinned at me.

"Wipe that dumb grin off your freckled face," I said as I balanced my way across.

"What y'all fussin' about?" Angel asked.

"Nothing." I said. "Now, move along, Buddy. We got to find Wallis."

When we caught up to Cotton, he said, "We'll go a little further along this ridge, but we won't come back this way. It'll be shorter to go down the side. That way, we won't have to cross the stream again."

"I'd sure like to come back here sometime," I said. "That's a great place to swim."

"You're right about that." Buddy punched my arm. I couldn't help but grin at him. I never could stay peeved at him for long. So he got to hold Angel's hand. So what? Heck, she kissed me.

"Let's go." Cotton said. He moved forward, and we followed. Ida Mae was getting tired, and as a matter of fact, so was I. As we moved along the ridge, the sound of the waterfall disappeared. Mockingbirds ran through endless cycles of birdsongs while chipmunks and squirrels chattered at us. The air was warm.

"I'm sleepy," Ida Mae said.

Angel took Ida's hand. "Maybe we should go back now. We haven't seen the Walking Man for a long time. In fact, I never saw him this morning."

"Well, he's got to be somewhere near here, because Maggie saw him come this way. Right?" Cotton looked at me.

I was not about to admit that I wasn't sure where Wallis had gone. "Yep," I said, "this is the way he came. Of course, we stayed in the water so long, we could have lost him."

"Can we look just a little more?" Cotton asked Ida.

"I guess so. If Angel wants to." Ida said.

Angel smiled. "Just a little more. Then we have to go, or Mom will get excited that we're not home for lunch."

When we moved ahead again, we heard voices, faint clanging sounds, and the rumble of an engine.

"I smell something peculiar," said Cotton. "Like rotten corn, maybe."

We all sniffed. "Me too," said Buddy.

"Now, Ida Mae, you be real quiet, hear?" Cotton patted Ida's head. "We're going over the ridge a bit. You stay here."

"Is the witch here?"

Cotton laughed. "Maybe, and maybe not."

"I'll stay by her," Angel said. "Y'all go on."

"You sure, Angel?" I asked. "Come on, she'll be okay." I wanted Angel to go with us.

"I'll be along in a minute. I'll stay by Ida until she's settled."

I was disappointed, but I knew that if Angel left, Ida would put up a fuss, then the game would end, so I moved along with the boys. I looked back once to see Angel talking to Ida and hugging her. Maybe this time she would leave the girl for a few minutes. I sure wished she would.

Cotton motioned for us to spread out. We separated into a line about ten yards away from one another. The trees were fewer, but the brush became heavier, so as we got closer to the noise, it was harder for us to see each other.

We were down the other side of the ridge now. Buddy should have been to my left and Cotton to my right, but I wasn't sure. I also didn't know exactly how far to go. I kept moving down the hill until I could see men working around a small shack. I crawled onto a boulder and lay down flat. I didn't have a clear view of what they were doing, but I could see parts of the small building, and once in a while, the men moved into sight.

Smoke billowed out a metal chimney on the roof of the shack. The smell of rotten corn was everywhere. Even though the trees and brush kept me from seeing the men clearly, I could hear snatches of what they said.

"Sometime tonight or early in the morning, this batch has to go over to Jefferson County."

"Who's drivin'?"

"Alton'll take a load."

My ears fairly exploded. *Alton.* That was Buddy's dad. And it wasn't like it was a common name. Now I just had to get a better view. I wiggled off the boulder and crept as quiet as I could down the hill.

I went maybe another twenty yards and slipped between some pine saplings. I peered out just as a woman came out of the shack. Dang, she sure was somethin'. Blond hair almost the color of Cotton's, only his was real. She wore a bright red dress with big gardenia flowers all over it. It was low-cut too, and she had the biggest tits I'd seen in a long time. In fact, I don't think I had ever seen any that big.

Anyway, she pranced around outside the shack, and then a man came out. Sure enough, it was Buddy's dad. Holy smokes. I hoped

Buddy couldn't see this. The other two men were nowhere to be seen. Alton ran his hands across the woman's breasts, and she squealed, "Alton, now stop that, or I'll tell on you."

"Who you goin' to tell?"

"Maybe I'll tell Mark, Jr. How'd you like that?"

"So you like him better than me?"

"I never said that," she said. "I like you both for different reasons. If you get my drift."

"Sure do. You like what's in my pants and what's in his wallet."

With that said, he undid his pants and whipped out his business. I couldn't help it. I screamed.

"What the hell?" Alton zipped his pants and looked my way.

The two other men ran out of the shack. One was skinny, and the other was a bearded fat man. He had a shotgun. Alton pointed in my direction, and the fat man cut loose. *Boom! Boom!* Buckshot rained down around me. I started up the hill in a hurry. Maybe they wouldn't see me in the brush.

Normally, I couldn't run fast, but when someone was chasing me with a shotgun, I could really move. I heard them coming behind me. I didn't know where the boys were, but I figured it was every man for himself. My plan was to go up and over the ridge as quick as I could.

When I got to the top, there stood Ida Mae, quiet as a mouse. "Where's Angel? We got to go, now."

"She went down to look for you."

I took a quick look around, but I didn't see anyone else. I figured Angel couldn't be far behind. When she got to the top and didn't see Ida Mae, she would know one of us had taken care of her. We always did.

"Come on, Ida. Let's go." I grabbed her hand and dragged her down the other side of the mountain. She was little, but she could run faster than me. Going down was easier than coming up, and the brush was not as thick. The closer we got to the bottom, the more the brush thinned out, until finally we were back on ground matted with pine needles.

I breathed a sigh of relief as we stepped out of the woods. I saw Cotton standing by the crossroad. He waved. His white hair was all matted with sweat and bits of brush.

As we walked over, Ida asked me, "Did you see the witch?"

"Sure did."

"Was you scared?"

"Sure was."

"Is that why you screamed?"

"Yep." I let go of Ida Mae's hand.

Cotton was all red in the face from running. "What the heck did you yell about?"

"She saw the witch," Ida said.

"I'll tell you later," I said. "Maybe."

"Dang, Maggie. You about got us killed."

Buddy stepped out of the woods. He was all dirty and muddy, his face about as red from running as the hair on his head. My face must have been red too, and from more than just running. I looked at my clothes. They were just as dirty as the boys'. Ida Mae still looked pretty clean.

Buddy said, "Golly, girl. You sure can holler! What'd you see?"

"Nothin'." I wasn't about to tell him. It would have embarrassed him something terrible. I loved Buddy like a brother, and I wouldn't hurt him.

"Well, y'all don't just holler to holler, now, do you?" Buddy wouldn't let it go.

"Come on, Maggie," Cotton said. "What happened? Good grief, when I heard those shots go off, I got real scared."

"She saw the witch," Ida offered.

Buddy stood with his arms crossed over his chest. I thought maybe he was mad, but then he smiled. "Did you see the witch?"

I didn't know what any of them saw, but since nobody said anything about Buddy's dad, I figured they hadn't gotten a look at him.

I got too much of a look myself. Maybe I would tell them, but for now, I couldn't. Anyhow, Ida Mae was there. She was too little to hear the details.

"I saw a man pee. That's all. Nothin' else."

Buddy's mouth dropped open. "What?"

"You must be kiddin'." Cotton said. "Screamin' like that over some guy peein'."

"Well, you weren't there. It startled me, that's all." I sounded as indignant as I could.

"I'll be darned." Buddy said. "About got us killed over some guy peein'!"

"She saw the witch. She saw the witch," Ida sang.

"Never mind," I said. "I'm taking Ida home. Angel must already be there, and I don't want to hear another word about it." I grabbed Ida Mae's hand and walked away. The boys started laughing. My face got red with anger, but I was damned if I was going to tell them anything now.

Ida Mae sang as we turned onto the paved road that ran through Taneytown. "Maggie saw the witch. Maggie saw the witch. He'll gobble you up and throw you in the ditch."

She was just too smart, that little Ida Mae.

CHAPTER 4

As we walked through town, Deeter came out of his store and yelled, "Don't forget, Maggie, I got your BB gun. And tell your dad I need to see him about a sign."

"I won't forget, Deeter. Me and Dad will be down, maybe tonight after supper. You gonna be open at six?"

"Sure thing. See you later."

I continued down Main Street for two short blocks and turned onto Oak Street. Angel and her family lived in a real nice house in the middle of the block. It was a white two-story with bright green shutters and two tall oak trees in the front yard. Roses grew along the picket fence that ran beside the sidewalk. Mrs. Albright, Angel's mom, loved to garden, but she spent most of her days keeping the house spotless—same as my mom. They knew one another, but I guess you couldn't exactly say they were friends, although sometimes they visited for coffee. Anyway, when Ida Mae and I walked up to the door, Mrs. Albright opened it like she'd been expecting us.

"Well, look at you, Maggie. My goodness, you sure must have been having fun."

I looked at my dirty shirt and jeans. "Yeah, we had fun."

"We were wading, and we saw the witch," Ida Mae said.

Mrs. Albright motioned us inside. "I do declare, Ida, you certainly have an imagination."

"We did. Tell her, Maggie."

I didn't want to tell Mrs. Albright anything about the morning—especially about the witch. As we walked to the kitchen, I said, "We did wade a little, but I'm not sure about the witch."

"You did too see the witch. You screamed. Cotton said so, and I heard you!"

I smiled slyly, and Mrs. Albright bought the deception. She said, "Now, Ida, we'll just forget about the witch. Run along and get cleaned up for lunch." She went over to the kitchen counter and started to make some sandwiches. "Where's Angel?" she asked.

"Gee, I thought she was here."

Mrs. Albright brushed a strand of her dark hair away from her face. "Why, no. I wondered why you were bringing Ida home."

My mind ran a mile a minute. "Angel said she wanted to come home to change her shoes because we were playing in the woods," I said. "Then we went wading in the Cahaba. I just thought she decided not to come back. I'm sure she'll be here soon."

"Is she playing with Buddy? I know she likes him."

My face reddened. "Maybe she is."

"Would you like some lunch?"

"No, ma'am. I have to get going. I have some chores to do; otherwise I won't get my allowance on Saturday."

"Well, you run along, then. I'm sure Angel will be here directly." She gave me a pat on the head as she walked me to the front door.

As I walked away, Ida shouted, "We saw the witch! We saw the witch! He gobbled us up and threw us in the ditch!"

I turned to look back and saw Ida was beside herself with giggles. She covered her mouth with her hands to stop the laughter, but it was no use. Her mom gently pulled her inside and shut the door.

I ran down the street and turned onto Main, hoping to find Angel, but she was nowhere to be seen. I flew past Sue Ann's grill and down to the cross street that ran alongside the river. Angel wasn't there. In spite of the snakes, I decided to go to Buddy's house to find out if he had seen Angel. I also needed to fill the boys in on the story I had told Mrs. Albright.

As I walked along the river road, an unfamiliar, high-pitched voice said, "Hello, missy."

I jumped. The Walking Man stepped out from behind a tree. He smiled at me. It was a crooked, thin-lipped, snaggletoothed smile. My eyes bugged out, and I stopped dead.

He tipped his black cowboy hat, and wads of brown and grey hair tumbled to his shoulders. He pushed up the hair and snugged the hat back on his head. "Bye, now." He turned and walked away at a fast pace. My mouth dropped open, but I couldn't scream.

"Holy shit," I whispered. I watched him disappear, then ran like heck to Buddy's house. Snakes wouldn't keep me away, not anymore. I had seen the witch up close, and I had lived.

"Buddy. Buddy!" I yelled. I flew up the porch steps and even forgot about the holes in the floor.

Mrs. Toliver came to the screen door with Buddy's youngest sister balanced on her hip. She brushed sweat from her forehead and pushed back her yellowish hair. "Buddy's doin' chores, Maggie. He can't play now."

"I just need to see him a minute, that's all."

"Well, honey, he's 'round back hacking weeds along the river edge. Now, mind, don't keep 'im away from his work, or his dad won't be happy with 'im."

I jumped off the porch. "I won't!" I knew what Buddy's dad would do if he had any kind of an excuse.

I rounded the back of the house and saw Buddy swinging the weed whacker back and forth in wide half-circles. The weeds flew in all directions. It was hot in the noontime sun, and Buddy was sweating like the devil. His face was beet red.

"Hey, Buddy!" I yelled to him.

He stopped swinging. "Hello, girl." He threw the weed whacker down and walked over. "Whatcha doin' here?"

"I just came from Angel's house, and she isn't home yet, and the Walking Man jumped out at me just down the street. And I didn't know what to tell Angel's mother when I brought Ida Mae home, and Angel wasn't there, and—"

Buddy cut me off. "Slow down, girl. You got too many things goin' round. I can't keep up. Now, what about Angel?"

"She wasn't home when I got there. She should have been."

"Well, that's odd. Of course, she's probably there now, so don't worry about it." Buddy asked, "Now, what about Wallis?"

"I was on my way here, and he jumped out at me from behind a tree and said, 'Hello, missy.' I about peed my pants."

Buddy laughed. "There sure is a lot of peein' today."

I got kind of indignant. "Don't start that again. This is serious stuff. Anyway, I didn't know what to say to Mrs. Albright, so I told her we were playing over here by your house and that we got wet wading in the river. Tell Cotton what I said."

"I will, but I don't see why you made up a story."

"Because we haven't ever been over the way we went, and we don't need anybody knowing about us bein' shot at."

"Well, that's true. My dad would skin me if he thought I was spyin' on people."

I wanted to say: *For sure, he'd skin you if he knew how close you came to spying on him.* I didn't say anything, though. I just shrugged.

"I got to go back to my chores, Maggie. I'll tell Cotton what to say if anybody asks, but I don't think nobody will." He turned back to whacking weeds. The sun glinted off the buckles of his overalls.

I watched him a minute before I left. I was hungry, so I figured I'd better go home. Plus I probably had chores of my own to do. Tonight after supper, my dad and I would go to Deeter's to get my BB gun. That thought made me smile.

I walked along the river road and headed through town. As I reached the macadam of Old Looney Mill Road, which headed up the hill towards my house, I started singing, "I saw the witch. I saw the witch. I gobbled him up and threw him in the ditch."

Dang that Ida Mae.

CHAPTER 5

When I got home, it was going on one o'clock. My brother Charlie stood on the porch steps, eating a sandwich. Our black-and-white cocker spaniel, Tinker, sat patiently waiting for a crumb to fall.

"Where you been?" Charlie asked.

"Nowhere." I walked up the steps. "What have you been doing?"

"Helping Dad with some signs. My work's done, and I get to go swimming. You still have work to do."

"Well, if you're going swimming, so am I."

"Maybe you will, and maybe you won't." He handed Tinker a corner of his sandwich. She wagged her tail as she gobbled up the morsel.

"Don't start with me, Charlie, or I'll tell Dad about you and Buddy slippin' down to the river at night to swim when you know you're not supposed to."

"Darn you, Maggie. Can't you take a little teasing? Don't tell Dad that."

"Well, don't tease me, then."

He grinned. "Mom's got a sandwich for you and some Kool-Aid. If you get your chores done, we can all go swimming. Hurry up. It's hot."

I loved my brother, but he could sure get my goat. Sometimes we fought like cats and dogs, but if anybody started something with either one of us, we'd jump in and fight like the dickens to help the other one. Other times, I for sure wanted to pop him. *When I get my BB gun,* I thought, *he'd better watch out with that teasing stuff.*

"Hey, Mom," I said as I went into the kitchen.

She turned from the kitchen sink. "Good heavens, Maggie. Where have you been? Just look at your clothes."

"Buddy, Cotton, and Angel and me went wading. Ida too."

"Well, goodness. Go get washed up, and sit down and eat. You have to do some ironing, and when you finish, we can go swimming."

I went into the bathroom and washed as quick as I could.

Mom said, "By the way, Mrs. Albright called and asked if Angel was here. I told her that neither one of you were here."

I got scared. "When did she call?"

"About ten minutes ago. She's getting worried about Angel. I understand you took Ida Mae home."

I sat down at the table and started eating, but my sandwich was hard to swallow. "We all were wading, and I thought Angel went home to change her shoes. She must be home by now."

Mom continued washing dishes. "Anyway, I told her to call back if Angel didn't get home within an hour. I'm sure she will, so I don't expect a call."

I fussed over my sandwich and drank my cherry Kool-Aid slow like. I had no idea why Angel wasn't home. I started thinking about the buckshot and the men running after us. I was sure it had something to do with Angel not getting home. I was working myself up with all sorts of images. My imagination ran wild. Where could she be?

I tried to act calm. "Deeter has my BB gun, Mom. He wants to see Dad about a sign. Maybe we could go down there after supper."

She hung the dish towel on a rack by the window, then sat down next to me. "I'm sure your dad will take you down. I know how much that BB gun means to you. Now finish up, honey, and get the ironing done. Charlie wants to go swimming, and you know Dad doesn't like you kids to swim in the river alone."

"I know." I drank the last swallow of Kool-Aid and rinsed the metal tumbler in the sink. I glanced at the kitchen clock. About ten minutes had passed since I got home. Time dragged, and I didn't want to hear the phone ring.

Mom went into the bathroom, got the ironing board for me, and brought it into the kitchen. "I'm going to visit a neighbor for a while," she said. "It'll take about thirty minutes to iron those shirts and pillowcases. I'll be back shortly."

"Okay." I pulled the basket of clothes from the corner and waited while the iron heated up. I really didn't mind ironing; in fact, I was pretty good at it. I heard the screen door slam shut and knew Charlie was coming my way.

"You done yet?"

"Dang you, Charlie! I haven't started. And if you keep it up, I'll take all afternoon, and we won't get to go swimming. So there."

He rummaged in the refrigerator and took an apple from a lower drawer. He crunched into it. "You sure are ornery today. What's up?"

"Nothin'." I wet my finger to test the iron. It sizzled. I pulled a pillowcase out of the basket and started working.

"Something's the matter. I can tell." He took another bite from the apple. Charlie always knew when something was bothering me. He would just keep after me until I told him. For once, there was no need to keep anything from him.

"I'm worried about Angel," I said.

"What about her?"

"We were all playing in the woods and wading in the river this morning, and she isn't home. I took Ida Mae home." I folded the ironed pillowcase and laid it on the counter.

"I don't think that's a big deal. She's probably there by now." He chomped another plug from the apple.

"Probably. Did you ever see the waterfall in the woods behind town?"

"Waterfall? You gotta be kidding. Where?"

"Well, if you go towards the river and turn right on the river road, then down to the willow tree near the bend, you'll find a sort of animal path. You follow that for maybe a mile up the mountain and along the ridge. Might be two miles, I don't know. Anyway, you can hear the waterfall." I finished pressing one of Dad's shirts and held it up. No wrinkles.

Charlie leaned on the counter. "Dang, Maggie. That's a long ways. You aren't kidding, are you? And when were you there?"

"Me and Cotton found it about a week ago. I'm not kidding, and if you don't believe me, I'll take you there tomorrow and show you, Mr. Smarty Pants. There's also a great swimming pool below the fall."

"Well, you can just do that. I'll be the judge of how great the swimming pool is." He tossed the apple core in the garbage. "And hurry up." He left. The screen door slammed behind him.

"Twenty minutes, and I'll be done!" I yelled. "Then we'll see who can stay underwater the longest."

While I ironed, I listened intently, praying that the phone wouldn't ring. I didn't want to know that Angel hadn't gotten home. I had a bad feeling. I couldn't think that anything would be wrong, yet my mind kept thinking about it.

The screen door creaked, and Mom said, "Are you done, Maggie?" She came into the kitchen.

"Yes, just finishing up."

"Run along and get your swimming suit on. I'll put things away. Then we'll go. Charlie is pacing about the front yard like a penned-up horse." She smiled. Her dark eyes shone.

"It'll take me a minute, Mom." I didn't need any more prodding. It was hot as heck, and all I wanted to do was to jump in the clean, clear water of the Cahaba. I wanted to forget everything about this morning and just stay underwater until Charlie yelled uncle. I'd show him a thing or two about underwater stuff.

When I came back to the kitchen, Mom had already put on her bathing suit. We headed out.

Charlie pranced up the hill ahead of us. He fairly ran down the other side. It was all I could do to keep from running away from Mom so I could keep up with him. At the bottom of the hill, the macadam ended. We made our way along a path through the brush, past the foundation of a long-abandoned mill, and came to the river.

The sandy bank sloped gently to the water's edge. Mom sat on a rock and pulled a book from her tote bag. The clear, cool water felt good. Charlie was already splashing in the rapids above the pool. The sun filtered through the oak and pine trees and cast great, green shadows on the water. It was beautiful.

In a moment, I forgot all about that morning and the buckshot and Angel. The sun moved toward the mountain we lived on, and the shadows lengthened. Mom swam for a while then went back to her reading. Charlie and I spent hours seeing who could swim underwater the longest, testing our lungs till they felt like they would pop.

Most of the time, I won. Then he would have one last test, and I would lose. He usually got to be the Grand Exalted Champion of Underwater just before it was time to go home. That day was no exception. I tried to hide my frustration, but inside I was mad as hell. Charlie always somehow got the best of me. A lot of people would give up, but it just made me more determined to one day be the High Mucky Muck.

"You cheat, Charlie."

He grinned. "It was fair and square. You agreed to one last swim for the Grand Exalted. I won. You're just sore because you lost." He ducked underwater.

"Well, you won't trick me anymore, Mr. Smarty Pants. You just wait."

Mom had had enough. "Come on. It's time to go."

I waded to shore and wrapped a towel around my waist. Charlie came up behind me, chanting, "Grand Exalted, that's me."

We began walking up the hill towards home. Charlie and I lagged behind Mom. "You know you cheat," I said.

Charlie grinned.

"I might tell Angel how you cheat."

"Now, why would you do that?" he asked.

"Because you like her."

"Maybe I do, but I like you too, Sis. We were just playin'." He put his arm across my shoulder and squeezed. "Don't be mad."

It was hard to stay mad at my brother. I forgot about being mad and thought about my BB gun and Angel. I knew I'd get my Daisy air rifle that night, but I wondered if Angel had gotten home. I was sure she had.

As we walked up the hill, Charlie and I chucked rocks at trees. He tried to get me to play for the King of Rock Chuck title, but I wasn't quite over the sting of the loss of the Underwater title, and I wouldn't agree. I for sure was not going to lose twice in one day, and that was that.

CHAPTER 6

Mom always had supper ready around the time Dad got home, and that night was no exception. He came in smelling of paint and gasoline. Speckles of different-colored paint spattered his bare arms and shirt.

"Hello, everybody." He smiled broadly. "I'll get cleaned up, so we can eat. I'm starved." He gave Mom a kiss on the cheek and headed for the bathroom.

Charlie sat at the table, while I helped Mom put food into the dishes. It was a mystery to me how she could fix all that stuff and have it ready at the same time, but I never pondered the subject too long. I was more interested in things like BB guns and my friends.

"Did Angel's mom call?" I asked.

"No. I haven't heard a thing, so everything must be all right." Mom placed the bowl of spaghetti and meatballs at the center of the table. "Now, put out the salad bowls while I get the bread."

By the time Dad came out of the bathroom, the table was set. It was like clockwork, even on weekends. If it was suppertime and me and Charlie were out playing, Dad would whistle for us, and supper would be ready, and it would be 5:30 PM. Clockwork.

That night, we spent time talking about what we had done during the day. Tinker sat at the end of the table, hoping for scraps. Dad had a strict rule about not feeding her while we ate, but sometimes Charlie slipped her food. It was just one more thing I could use on him, if I had to.

"Deeter wants to see you about a sign, Dad. And he has my Daisy air rifle. And I have my money saved."

"Well, that's three good things. When should we take care of this?"

I saw him wink at Mom. She tried to smile, but I knew she didn't like the idea of me having a BB gun. "Maggie would like to go this evening," she said.

"Could we? Please?" I asked.

"We can do that, Maggie. Tonight will be our night." He turned to Charlie. "You help your mother clean up, and then tomorrow night, you and I will go fishing."

Charlie screwed up his face. I wanted to laugh, but I didn't dare. This was one of those rare times when Charlie had to help with dishes. I'd give him a horse laugh later, but I was afraid that if I did it now, Dad wouldn't take me to Deeter's, and I wanted that gun more than anything.

"No faces, Charlie. And Maggie, don't you laugh." Dad never missed a lick.

It felt strange not doing the dishes, but I liked the freedom of eating and then doing what I wanted. This was better than Grand Exalted. Dad had his back to me while he kissed Mom, so I smirked at Charlie. He glared back.

I felt pretty smart as Dad and I drove down Old Looney Mill Road in our station wagon towards Taneytown. I cranked the window down to let in the breeze. The town was quiet. A few cars had parked around Sue Ann's grill, and some were down by the movie house, but there was nothing in front of Deeter's. It looked like it might be closed, but as we pulled in, Deeter came out the door.

He gave Dad his ragged-toothed smile and extended his hand. "Glad you came, John. But I guess the little one wanted her BB gun real bad. The sign don't matter that much to 'er." He spit a wad of juice into the gutter.

Dad smiled as he shook Deeter's hand. "No, it's not about the sign. Let's get the BB gun out of the way. Then you and I can talk about what you need."

We followed Deeter into the store. He turned on one light as he walked towards the cash register. The gun was lying cross ways on the counter, and my heart skipped. The wood stock was shiny, and the carved Red Ryder name stuck out real plain. Two blue and white tubes of BBs lay next to it.

Dad inspected it carefully. "Well, Maggie, this is a good-looking Daisy. It's what you want, huh?"

"More than anything."

He handed it to me. "Now, remember—this is not a toy. It can hurt real bad to get hit with a BB."

I felt the smoothness of the metal barrel and the wood forearm and stock. The leather saddle strap made the gun look just like one that Roy Rogers used. I aimed at one of the stuffed pheasants suspended from the ceiling.

"Well, you got your part. Where's mine?" Deeter grinned as he held out his hand.

"Huh?" I lowered the gun.

"You're buyin' it, ain't you?" Deeter winked at Dad. "A deal's a deal."

"I sure am. I got my money right here." I leaned the gun against the counter and dug into my jeans pocket. I pulled out some bills and a wad of change that must have weighed two pounds. As it spilled all over the counter, I said, "There."

Deeter counted out the money careful like. "It looks like you have four dollars and eighty-two cents here. That's short by thirteen cents."

"No, it can't be!" I had visions of losing my Daisy. I dug in my pockets again, but there was no more money. I felt tears trying to come. I'd be damned if I'd cry, but this was serious. I looked at my Dad.

"Well," Dad said, "we have to live up to the bargain, so I'll chip in the rest." He counted out thirteen cents from his change. "This will have to come out of this week's allowance, Maggie."

"I know. Thanks, Dad."

"You run along outside while Deeter and I talk." He patted my head.

I didn't need any more prodding. I grabbed the packets of BBs and ran into the night. Deeter's side of the street had a few more cars, and tons were parked along the other side by Sue Ann's. The café was loaded with more people than I had ever seen in there. Mixed in with the other cars by Sue Ann's was Chief Dinsdale's police car. I clutched my Daisy tight as I crossed the street.

I peered in through the front window. Dinsdale was talking to the folks inside. They were drinking coffee but mostly just listening to whatever he was saying. I didn't see any kids, so I sure wasn't going in there by myself.

"Maggie? Is that you?"

I jumped at the voice. Deputy Bob walked up. "Hi," I said.

"Say, now, little girl. Are you packin' that rifle for a reason?" He loomed large above me.

"No. I plan on playing with it. You know, shoot mistletoe off the trees and stuff like that."

He smiled. "Well, come on inside. The chief wants to talk to you."

My mouth dropped open. I hadn't had my gun ten minutes, and already Chief Dinsdale wanted to talk to me. Damn. "I didn't do anything. Honest."

Deputy Bob put his hand on my shoulder and guided me towards the entrance.

As he opened the squeaky screen door, the buzz inside subsided. I didn't want to go, but I had no choice. Dinsdale saw us and motioned us up front.

"Howdy, Miss Maggie. I been lookin' for you. Your mom said you came downtown to get your gun." He smiled. "See you got it."

I knew he didn't want to talk to me about my BB gun, but I sure couldn't imagine what else there was. "Yeah," I said. I felt trapped. The crowd was real quiet, just staring at us. I clutched my Daisy close. "I haven't done anything, Mr. Dinsdale."

"I reckon I know that, but I need to ask about what you did this morning. You and Buddy, Cotton, Ida Mae, and Angel. Especially Angel."

"We didn't do nothin'. Just kid stuff. You know." All sorts of things ran through my mind. "Did you talk to Buddy?"

"Sure did. He says you went wadin' in the river. Is that true?"

Oh, bless Buddy. He remembered. "Yeah, that's what we did. The boys went swimmin', but not me or Angel. I waded some with Ida Mae, but Angel never went into the water. She had on good shoes, and I think she went home to get some other ones."

"Ida Mae had a different story about climbing a mountain and followin' the Walkin' Man." He placed his hand on my shoulder. "How about that?"

Just then, the door to the café opened with a bang. Dad walked in. "What's up, Chief?" he asked.

"Hi, John. We have a little problem here in town, and I thought maybe Miss Maggie could help."

Dad looked down at me. "Well, tell Chief Dinsdale what he wants to know."

"Yes, sir." I got scared. I knew something was wrong, but I wasn't going to tell about the scene in the woods with the shotgun. Buddy would get skinned if his dad knew we were anywhere near that whiskey still. I had to lie. It was the only way.

"Now, what were you sayin', Miss Maggie?"

I gave the chief my most sincere look. "We all went wading in the river. Honest. Ida Mae just makes up stories like mad. She's always seeing ghosts and stuff. Ask Angel. She'll tell you."

The sheriff bit his lower lip. He looked at my dad, then down at me. "That's the problem, Miss Maggie. Miss Angel is missing. I thought maybe you could help."

It felt like my heart stopped. "What? But that can't be. She always goes home."

"Not this time, Miss Maggie. Not this time." He pushed his tan Stetson back on his head and sighed. He spoke to my dad. "That's all I wanted to know, John. You and Maggie can go now."

Dad and the chief exchanged looks but said nothing. The crowd fidgeted with spoons and coffee cups. I felt like my heart would just break. My face was burning, and my hand felt sweaty on the cold metal of my Daisy.

As Dad and I neared the front door, Chief Dinsdale called, "If you remember anything, let me or the deputy know."

"I will," I said.

The sticky night air made my face feel hotter. Dad walked beside me to the station wagon and opened the door. I slid across the soft fabric seat and felt tears come to my eyes. Dad started the engine and backed out onto Main Street. He drove down towards the river while I stared out the window at the dark brick buildings. The movie house marquee was lit, and people were coming out of the lobby, laughing and talking. As we drove by, I could smell the lingering odor of popcorn. I busted out sobbing.

"Don't cry, Maggie." Dad pulled me close. I felt the warmth of his body and smelled the familiar mixture of gasoline and paint. I should have felt safe, but for some reason, I didn't. I somehow knew that I would never find what I had lost on that day. Where could she be? Angel. My Angel.

CHAPTER 7

I did not sleep well that night. My Daisy lay next to me, and many times, I rolled on top of it. The cold, steely hardness woke me upright. Each time, I sat looking at the darkened room, fearing something under my bed. But I was too afraid to look, so I lay down again and drifted in and out of sleep. Once, I cocked my gun and fired under the bed, just to make sure nothing was there. I felt safe when there was no scream. Toward morning, I must have slipped into a deep sleep.

"Maggie, Maggie!" Charlie pushed my arm. "Get up, girl. It's almost nine o'clock."

"Huh?" I rolled over and faced him.

"Dang. You look terrible. What's the matter?"

"Nothin'."

He sat on the edge of the bed. "It's about Angel, isn't it?"

I gritted my teeth and fought back tears. "Yeah. Has anybody said anything about her bein' home?"

"No. But don't worry. Lots of folks are out looking. They think maybe she got lost in the woods somewhere. Dad took off work today, and he's with a bunch of people over by the river park."

I knew Charlie was the only one I could tell about yesterday, but I didn't want to tell him yet. He might tell Dad, and I had lied to Dad and the police chief. I didn't want to lose Dad's trust. Angel had to get home. She just had to. "You still want to go see the water-fall?" I asked.

"Yeah, that's why I came in your room. Mom said not to bother you, but heck, you've been sleeping long enough for two people." He stood. "Get dressed, girl."

After he left, I pushed my legs over the edge of the bed and sat staring out my window. I thought of Mozell then, the old colored woman who lived in a little shack of a house on the bottoms across the river. Mozell was wise. Maybe she could help me decide what to do. I determined that I would go see her in the afternoon. Some-how, thinking of her made me feel better.

Mom stuck her head in my doorway. "You ready for breakfast now, sleepyhead?" She smiled at me.

"Sure, Mom. What are we havin'?" I started to dress.

"You can have whatever you want this morning. Afterwards, you and Charlie need to just go play." Then, in a stricter voice, she added, "But not by the river."

"We weren't thinkin' of going there." I pulled a knit shirt over my head and tucked it into my jeans. "Can I have some eggs and toast?"

"Of course." She came into the room and hugged me tight. I looked into her dark eyes and thought I saw a tear, but I wasn't sure. She kissed my cheek, then left the room. Sometimes parents are hard to figure out. Mom never let me sleep so late. I guessed she was worried about Angel too.

I tied tight bows in my Keds and made my bed. One thing I knew: Mom might be worried about something, but you always had to make your bed. Today would be no exception. The white chenille cover was so tight you could bounce a quarter on it. I picked up my Daisy and headed for the kitchen.

"Mrs. Albright called this morning." Mom placed my eggs and toast on the table and sat down. "Now, Maggie, are you telling everything you know?"

"Sure, Mom. I told Chief Dinsdale everything about what we did." I put ketchup on my eggs and pushed them around my plate. The ketchup smeared blood red.

Charlie came into the kitchen, followed by Tinker. She sat down by me and waited for scraps. Charlie asked, "Are you ready yet?"

"She'll be ready in a moment." Mom stood and looked at me. "You've told everything?"

"Yeah, Mom. Why do you ask?"

"Ida Mae is insistent about following the Walking Man and finding a waterfall. Mrs. Albright is beginning to believe her."

Charlie was standing behind Mom. He gave me a funny, screwed-up face. I glared back with a look that told him to keep quiet.

"Mom, Ida Mae makes up all sorts of stories. She even thinks the Walking Man is a witch." I jammed the rest of my eggs and toast into my mouth. "That's how she thinks. Can Charlie and I go play now?"

Mom picked up my plate and glass. "All right, Maggie. Did you make your bed?"

"You know I did. You can even bounce a quarter on it, just like the Marines at Iwo Jima." I picked up my Daisy.

That made Mom laugh. "Your uncle Ed talks too much about the war. Go on, now. You and Charlie remember—stay away from the river."

"We will."

Charlie got outside before I did. He carried his Daisy, resting the barrel on his shoulder. "What's going on, Maggie? Sounds like Ida Mae isn't making up stuff."

We began walking down the hill towards Taneytown. "Don't you say nothin', Charlie. If you do, I'll tell Dad about you and Buddy swimming at night."

"Dang, would you let that go?"

"Well, don't say anything about the waterfall. Got it?"

"Okay. What's the big deal?" He cocked his Daisy and fired at a twig on an oak tree. The branch cracked and floated downward, leaves fluttering.

"There's no big deal. I don't want Dad to know about the waterfall yet." I cocked my rifle and shot at a small branch. The BB whistled through the air.

Charlie laughed. "Want to have a contest? See who can shoot branches off the trees the most?"

"Not yet. I just got my gun. You wait. I'll show you who can shoot the best."

"Well, you won't show me today."

We neared town. There weren't many cars along Main Street. The Walking Man was sitting on a bench outside Sue Ann's grill. He tipped his hat as we walked by. I moved closer to Charlie. I glanced back over my shoulder once or twice to see what the Walking Man was doing, but he just sat there like he was basking in the sun. Really odd. "How can he stand to have all those clothes on in this heat?" I asked.

Charlie glanced back at him. "I don't know. Maybe he's cold. He sure does like black. Man, everything he has on is black."

"I'll bet his underwear is black."

Charlie busted out laughing. "You say the dumbest things, Maggie. Black underwear. Oh, boy."

We reached the river road, and could see people wandering along both banks of the Cahaba. There were even men in boats dragging some sort of lines in the water. Charlie stopped to look.

"What are they doing?" I asked.

"I think maybe … oh, never mind. I don't know." He started walking towards the willow at the bend. "Come on, Maggie. Show me the waterfall. I'll bet you made that up."

I jumped into action. "I did not, Mr. Smarty. You'll see." I caught up to him. I swung my Daisy out in front of me and aimed at a twig on a maple tree. *Bam.* The BB whistled a tune through the foliage.

Charlie rolled his green eyes. "Aw. You got me."

I couldn't help but laugh. We were at the willow by then. "This way, Charlie."

I stepped off the dirt road onto the soft pine needles. The smell of the pine trees was wonderful. Sunlight sifted through the tall trees and made a patchwork of light and dark spots. I jumped along, trying to avoid the dark patches.

"What are you doing?" Charlie asked.

"Nothing. I'm just playing a dumb game."

"You want to play for a championship?"

"Geez, Charlie." I stopped jumping and stood in a shaft of light. "You make everything a competition. I'm not doing this anymore today, so don't try to start something about championships." I gave him my best mean look.

"Okay, Sis. I quit."

"Now, follow me." I walked along the animal trail, with Charlie following behind. We didn't talk for some time. Once in a while, Charlie fired off a round, and somewhere in the distance, the BB would find its mark. Mostly, we were quiet. As we started up the foot of the mountain, I was surprised to see a crow hopping around a shiny object on the ground. It must have heard us, because it suddenly flew right at me, cawing real loud. I stumbled backward.

"What the heck?" Charlie dropped his Daisy and struggled to keep his footing and to keep me from falling. "Dang, girl. You made me drop my gun."

"Well, I couldn't help it. It's not every day you get attacked by a crow. Why didn't you shoot it?"

"I don't shoot crows. It's bad luck, and you know it." He inspected the gun for damage. "Well, at least the Daisy isn't hurt."

I moved to where the crow had been and knelt down. I couldn't believe it. The shiny object was Angel's gold cross. The chain was missing.

"What is it?" Charlie asked.

"This is Angel's." I stood up. It made no sense to me.

"Let me see." He looked at the cross, then handed it back. "Are you sure?"

"Yes, I'm sure. I've seen this a million times. I know it's hers."

"Well, what's it doin' here?"

"Dang, Charlie. I'm no mind reader. I don't know. We came this way yesterday, and I guess she just lost it."

"I thought you told Mom and Dad you were down by the river yesterday."

Good night, nurse, I thought. I couldn't remember anything. Now I had let the cat out of the bag. Charlie would hold this over me forever. "So what? I wanted to keep our trip a secret. Now you know."

He pushed his cheek out with his tongue and arched his eyebrows. "I see. This should be worth something."

"Don't you start, mister. I got things on you too." I put the cross in my jeans pocket and started up the mountain. "We got a ways to go to the waterfall, so don't lag behind." I was mad at myself, and he knew it.

He laughed. "You're gonna get caught tellin' stories. It always happens. Mom and Dad always find out."

"Just be quiet, Charlie. If you don't, I won't take you any farther."

He stopped talking, so I plodded ahead. I carried my Daisy in my left hand, and my right was in my pocket, fingering the cross. It scared me. It shouldn't have been there in the woods. Angel had worn that cross every day for years. She would never be careless enough to lose it. I had a bad feeling. Something wasn't right, but I didn't know what. And where was Angel?

CHAPTER 8

It must have taken another thirty minutes for us to crest the mountain. The going was rough in the summer heat. When we got to the top, I stopped and sat on the narrow trail.

"Dang, Maggie, how far is this waterfall? You're pulling my leg." Charlie sat, facing me.

"I am not. You'll see. It isn't much further."

"It better be good. That was a hard climb." He cocked his gun and fired at something behind me.

"That's it! You just about shot my ear off. I'm not resting here any longer." I moved along the trail again. I fingered the cross in my pocket, thinking that Angel would be glad that I had found it.

"Hold up a minute, Sis." Charlie caught up to me.

"What were you shooting at?" I asked.

"A bird."

"A bird?" I turned to look at him. "I'm tellin' Dad. You know you're not supposed to do that."

"It was only a blue jay. They're mean to other birds. Eatin' their eggs and destroying their nests."

"Well, everybody knows that. That still doesn't give you the right to kill them." I didn't like blue jays either, but I sure wouldn't shoot one.

"I missed, anyway."

"I don't believe that, mister. You don't miss anything you shoot at. You better not do it again, or I'll tell Dad, and he'll take your gun."

"Okay. You don't tell Dad, and I won't tell about the waterfall. If we ever get there."

We walked in silence for some time and then started down. I stopped when I heard the waterfall. "Hear it?" I asked.

"Dang, I do hear something that sounds like falling water."

"I guess I wasn't kidding about this."

"Guess not."

"You can go first now, Charlie. I already got the surprise of seeing it yesterday. It's not far."

He broke into a run. I had trouble keeping up with him, and once we neared the turn, I slowed down. I knew he'd see it real soon.

He let out a whoop. "Dang, you weren't kiddin.'" He kept going, but before I got to the turn, he let out another kind of a cry. "Oh, no. Oh, no!"

"What is it?" The sound of his voice scared me. "Stop playin' with me, Charlie." I rounded the curve and started down.

Charlie was at the bottom already. The crashing of the water kept me from hearing what he was yelling, but I saw the pink dress and knew at once that he was standing near Angel. I was frantic. Charlie held out his hands to stop me from getting closer. "No, don't, Maggie. Don't go there."

"But I have to. Angel's hurt and needs my help."

He locked his arms around me. "We can't help her now."

"What do you mean? Of course we can."

He squeezed me tighter. "No, we can't, Maggie. It's too late. I think she's dead."

I felt the blood drain from my face. "No, no. It can't be. You're wrong. It can't be." I went limp then. I guess the heat and Charlie's message got to me, because everything went black.

I don't know how long I was out, but when I opened my eyes, my brother was wiping my forehead with his wet shirt. I was lying on the ground about twenty feet from Angel. Charlie knelt beside me. "You okay, Maggie?"

"I think so. Are you sure about Angel?" I felt tears in my eyes.

He stopped wiping my forehead. "I'm sure. We've got to get help."

"I'm not leaving her here all alone." I sat up and stared in her direction.

"There's nothing you can do, Maggie. We have to go." He pleaded.

"I'm telling you, I'm not leaving. You can go, but I am not leaving."

He must have sensed that I wouldn't leave, because he shrugged and patted me on the head. "You'll be all right?"

"Sure, Charlie. Sure. I'll stay by her."

"Don't touch nothin'. Hear?" He moved a few steps away.

"I won't. Go on now and hurry."

Charlie turned and ran up the mountain. I watched him until he disappeared among the pines and brush. Then I looked at Angel. I was scared, I admit it, but I felt so bad. I fingered my BB gun. Damn. I would never get to show it to her.

She looked so small lying by the water. Her hair was all muddy, and dirt and red smears covered her pink dress. I couldn't make myself go any closer. I sat where Charlie had left me and waited, and watched, and studied what I could. I couldn't see the golden necklace. I felt the cross in my pocket. "Angel," I said.

There was no answer. I knew there wouldn't be, but I had hoped. Above the sound of the waterfall, I heard a blue jay call its loud cackle. I got mad. Mad as hell.

"Damn you, you lousy baby killer. Don't you fly near me, or I'll shoot you. I'll kill you. Damn you."

The jay fluttered through the woods and I fired a shot. It continued flying. I started crying—sobbing and wailing like a baby. I just couldn't help it. I loved Angel, and she was gone forever, and I didn't even get to say good-bye. How would I ever explain this to Ida Mae? Or Buddy?

I tried to figure out what to tell them. She must have come back this way and then fell from the log above the falls, but that didn't account for the cross in the woods down the other side of the mountain. It made no sense. I couldn't think of what to say to anybody. I pulled the cross out of my pocket and turned it over and over, studying it real close. It was hers. I didn't know what it meant, but I knew I wouldn't tell anybody about it unless Charlie told. If he didn't, then it would be our secret. I would have something of Angel's. I would keep it always.

I don't know how long I waited, but while I sat watching over Angel, I decided that Mozell would be able to help me. She would know what to make of all of this, and maybe she could help me figure out what to say to Ida Mae and Buddy. I made up my mind that I would go see her as soon as I got home.

I was still thinking about Mozell when dark shadows moved across the sunlight. Vultures were circling over the pines. I got real scared then. I cocked my Daisy and waited. I would kill every last one of them if they even got near Angel. They circled and circled until the sky was a whirl of dark and light. Just like pinwheels. Pinwheels.

"Maggie. Maggie!"

I jumped up. Charlie and a bunch of men were running down the trail. Chief Dinsdale struggled to keep up. He yelled, "Don't touch nothin'. Don't touch nothin'! Stand clear!"

CHAPTER 9

Charlie and me walked up the trail after the chief, and the state police and all the other men got down to the pool. I took one last look at Angel. Then time sped up, and we were down at the river road. Deputy Bob was standing alongside the chief's car. "Hello, Miss Maggie. You okay?"

I looked at Deputy Bob and didn't know what to say. I wasn't okay, and I knew that it would never be the same again, but I couldn't explain how I felt, so I just nodded.

He patted me on the head. "It'll be all right. Y'all go on now."

The men who had been out on the river were alongside the bank, sitting in the rowboats, smoking and talking in low tones. The sun was hot, and red dust whirled in the soft summer breeze. I didn't look directly at anybody. I figured they knew I had been with Angel when Charlie came for help, and I didn't want to talk about any of it. We walked in silence to the paved stretch of Main Street.

"You got anything you want to tell me?" Charlie asked.

"No." I kicked at loose stones. "One thing, though. This is a special favor. You got to promise you won't tell anyone."

"What is it?"

"Did you tell anyone about the cross?"

"No, not yet."

"Promise me, then. Don't tell nobody about it. Please."

"Why not, Maggie? Angel's mother will want it."

"Please, Charlie. It's the only thing I got left of her." I felt the tears start. I reached out and touched Charlie's arm. "Please."

Charlie was silent for some time. We passed the movie house and Sue Ann's grill. Deeter stood on the sidewalk and watched us go by, but he didn't say anything. Randal was out in front of Deeter's, painting his Crosley coupe. Last week's green was being replaced with a coat of bright red. Even the stupidity of that didn't make me smile.

"What do you say, Charlie? Will you promise to keep it secret?"

He sighed. "All right, Maggie. I promise."

I reached inside my jeans and turned the cross over and over. For a time, Angel would still be with me. "Thanks."

As we passed by Oak Street, I looked to see if Mrs. Albright was outside. I was scared to see her. I had lied something awful to a lot of people. I couldn't imagine how she would feel when she found out about Angel. Now she would know that I had lied about us wading in the Cahaba. I still didn't know what I would tell her. Maybe she wouldn't ask me anything.

Me and Charlie started the long trek up Old Looney Mill towards home. The paved road had turned to gravel macadam. The tar oozed out in spots. I hated the tar, but sometimes Cotton would pull up a plug and chew it like gum. His teeth would get black, but he'd work at it while it cooled in his mouth and formed a little ball. Eventually, he'd throw the wad out across the fields.

I don't know why I thought of that as we walked along. Maybe because Angel always got so distressed when he did it. I figured Cotton did it to impress Angel, but it never did. Angel was above being impressed by dumb stuff like that. Angel was beyond being impressed by anything anymore. I got mad then. I was mad. Mad at God. Just mad. Then I stepped in a wad of gooey tar. "Damn it all to hell."

Charlie stopped in his tracks. "Calm down, Maggie. If Mom hears you talk like that, she'll whip you good."

"I don't care. I just don't care. Look at my shoe. Damn ol' Keds. I wish they were Mary Janes. Just like Angel's." I started crying and couldn't stop.

Charlie took my Daisy and put both guns in his left hand. His right arm went around me, and he let me rest my head on his shoulder. I was bawling for all I was worth as we reached the top of Old Looney Mill.

"Come on, Maggie. We're home now. It'll be okay." He led me across the ditch and into the front yard.

Mom came out onto the porch. "Oh, Maggie. Oh, Maggie." She squeezed me real tight, like she would never let me go.

"I'm tired," I said. "That's all. I'm tired."

"Of course you are. You need to rest for a while." She led me into to my bedroom. "You sleep for a little bit, and you'll feel better."

I pulled off my Keds and sat on my bed. "I'm sorry about the tar, Mom. I didn't mean to bring it inside."

"Never mind. We'll tend to that later."

"When I get up, I want to go see Mozell. I want to see her real bad."

"We'll see, Maggie. Maybe you can."

I drifted off then. I don't remember ever feeling that tired. Or that scared. Or that lonely.

CHAPTER 10

I dreamed of Angel. She was walking in the woods, and her Mary Janes were covered with mud, and she was crying. I tried to comfort her, but she kept crying. She kissed my cheek, and then I woke up. I went into the kitchen, where Mom was stirring batter for a cake.

"Why, honey," she said, "you've hardly slept."

"I know. I thought I was tired, but I guess I'm not. Can I go see Mozell?"

She held the metal bowl in her hand and continued stirring. "Are you all right?"

"Sure, Mom. Can I go see Mozell? Please?"

She set the bowl on the counter and put her arms around me. "You can go for an hour, but you need to get home then. The cake will be done, and you can have some. It's your favorite chocolate cake."

I managed a smile.

"Your shoes are out on the porch. Charlie cleaned the tar off for you. Now, run along and enjoy your visit with Mozell."

I went out on the porch. Charlie was sitting on the edge, with Tinker by his side.

"Thought you were going to sleep forever," he said.

"No, I wasn't. Anyway, I'm going to go see Mozell." I sat down to put on my Keds. I could smell the gasoline Charlie had used to clean the rubber soles. "Thanks for cleaning my shoes."

"Yeah. You owe me."

"Maybe I do, and maybe I don't."

"You do." He petted Tinker. "I got your Daisy. You want it?"

"I'll get it later. Bye, Charlie."

I went down the hill behind our house as fast as I could. Pine and oak trees were everywhere, but over time, I had worn a small path from our house over several small hills to the river road. I thought this was quicker than going through town. Besides, I didn't want to see anybody. I sure didn't want to see Chief Dinsdale.

When I came out of the woods, the boats and the men who had been out on the Cahaba were gone. I was glad. I ran for the bridge. Cotton was leaning against one of the railings. "Hey, girl. What happened? What happened to Angel?"

I was surprised to see him. "I don't know. I guess she fell from the log at the top of the falls." I could feel tears starting.

Cotton slowly chucked rocks into the river. "It ain't goin' to be the same."

"I know. Does Buddy know?"

"Probably. It's all over town. You can't keep any secrets in Taneytown." He threw another rock.

"Did Chief Dinsdale talk to you?" I asked.

"Yeah, yesterday."

"What'd you tell him?"

"I lied about where we went wading, if that's what you mean. I told him what Buddy said you wanted us to say." Cotton chucked another rock in the river.

"Maybe we won't have to talk to him anymore. We should just keep to our story." I said.

"I suppose. It won't change anything, anyway. Not now." He turned towards me.

I could see tears in his eyes, but he was too proud to let them fall in front of me. I wouldn't embarrass him by saying anything. "See you later, Cotton."

"Sure thing, Maggie. Be careful, girl." He tried to smile, but sadness clouded his blue eyes.

I crossed the bridge and turned south down Highway 280. I ran along the edge of the paved road for about a hundred yards before crossing to the other side. A narrow dirt road led into the bottoms where the river used to overflow before they put in the highway. Big drainage tubes funneled floodwater into this area sometimes, but mostly it was just good ol' black dirt mixed with red clay.

As I walked, a mockingbird called. The field in the bottoms had been planted with corn, and the stalks were almost as high as my head. The sun beat down, and I felt the sweat form on my forehead. I looked at the sky. It was full of white clouds and swirling with crows. It made me happy, and it made me sad.

Just past the cornfield, trees lined the road. Soon I was in the wooded part of the bottoms. On my left, a small stream flowed towards the river. It looked cool, but I never stepped in, because it was full of water moccasins and leeches. I hurried along another several hundred yards to where Mozell's small cabin sat among the trees on the right. As I approached, I could see that she was out on the swing, barely moving.

"Mozell!" I yelled.

She jerked, then laughed her rolling belly laugh. "You done scared me, honey girl. Dis ol' lady bin sleepin'."

I ran up the wooden steps and flung myself into her arms.

"My goodness, child. You are sweatin', and yet you's feel cold." She pushed me back, so she could look into my eyes. "What's goin' on?"

"Oh, Mozell. It's awful."

"You mean about Miss Angel?"

"You know?"

"Course I does. This here town ain't that big, and folks knows everything real quick-like."

I sat down on the swing beside her. She covered my hands with her wrinkled brown hands and stroked softly. When I leaned against her bosom, she pulled me tight. "I'm scared, Mozell."

"What y'all scared of?"

"I don't know. I'm just scared."

Mozell didn't say anything for some time. She just held me and moved the swing back and forth. I felt warm and secure. I studied the tiny flowers on her cotton dress. She wore a small gold band on the ring finger of her left hand. The ring looked worn and old. Still, it glistened in the sunlight that danced through the trees.

"I knows how you feel, Maggie. I done lost plenty of folks that I cared about. I's lost a husband and sons and friends. Life's that way. Y'all's young and maybe too young to lose a friend, but God has his plan. It ain't always clear, but God ain't never mean. Angel's wid him now. You can be sure."

"I'm not sure of that."

"Well, child. I done know it's true. Y'all just has to believe."

Mozell was so sure of her religion. I learned a long time ago that she would never doubt anything about God, but I wasn't so sure. It seemed mean to me, but I didn't say so. "I'll try to believe, Mozell. I'll try."

She patted my arm. "I's made some cookies dis mornin'. Y'all want some?"

I looked at her round face and dark-brown, twinkling eyes. I couldn't help but smile at her.

She laughed. "Run inside. They's in the tin. Oatmeal raisin."

Inside the small cabin, the wood-burning stove wasn't hot, but I could see where she had stacked some small logs alongside it on the floor, and I could smell the faint odor of burnt wood. The room was still hot from the morning baking. The green bread tin sat on a table in the middle of the room that was both kitchen and living room. The tin was heavy. "Should I bring the tin outside?" I called.

"Might as well. I may want some too."

As I stepped out, the screen door slammed behind me. I put the tin between Mozell and me, then struggled to pull the top off the box. Mozell laughed. "Jist like Joshua. Always strugglin' wid dat lid."

"It's hard to do," I said.

She took the tin and popped off the lid. The cookies were big and full of raisins. We both took one. She left the lid off, so I knew I could have more. "How come Joshua struggled with the lid?" I asked.

"That man's hands was big. I specks they got so big from liftin' that shovel and throwin' coal in the steel furnace. He jist fussed wid it, and his big ol' hands got in da way."

"Was that when you lived in Birmingham?" I chewed the last of the cookie and reached for another.

"Yes. Slagtown." She looked out across the road, and I saw her eyes mist. "He would fuss about it, but he loved that ol' green bread tin. I's pack his lunch in it. He tole me that his lunch was always fresh, and he owned it was because of the tin. When he got kilt by the train one night, he throwed it, and Percy, his friend, found it and brought it to me." She sighed. "That's when I's had enough of Birmingham. Thank the lord my kids was all growed."

"You still miss Joshua?"

She rubbed her eyes. "Not a day don't go by that I don't think of 'im. I ain't never cared about no man before or since Joshua."

"That's how I feel about Angel. I love her, Mozell." I couldn't chew the cookie, because my throat felt funny.

"Course you do, honey child." She moved the tin to her lap and pulled me close.

"I did something bad, Mozell."

"Now, I find that hard to believe. What's so bad?" She continued to hold me.

"I told a lie."

"A lie? 'Bout what?"

"About where Angel and me and Buddy and Cotton and Ida Mae went the day Angel disappeared."

"Now, why would you do that? Did you go somewheres you weren't supposed to?"

"Not really. But ... well, there was something I saw that I didn't want to tell about. And then something happened that scared us all, and we ran. I couldn't find Angel, but I thought she'd get home."

"Well, who'd you lie to?"

"Angel's mom. My mom. My dad. And Chief Dinsdale."

"Lordy be, girl. You sure picked the wrong folks to lie to." She pulled away and lifted my face. "What'd you tell 'em?" Her dark eyes studied mine.

"I told them we went wading in the river."

"Well, where were ya?" Mozell let go of my face and leaned back on the swing.

"We were up the mountain, and we found a waterfall, and we were wading and fooling around there."

"That don't sound so bad. What scared ya?" Mozell patted my hand.

"I don't want to tell that part, because the rest of it would hurt my friend Buddy."

"Hmm. I see. Well, what did Buddy and Cotton tell?"

"I made them promise to say we went wading in the river, and that's what they did. All except Ida Mae."

"Ida Mae. So what did that little child say?" Mozell rocked the swing slow like.

"She said we got scared by a witch and that I screamed."

Mozell gave a belly laugh. "Well, I declare. Did that happen?"

"No, not all of it. I did scream, though."

"You did? What for?"

"I saw something that made me scream. It wasn't no witch."

"Was it a snake, or what?" She stopped rocking and looked at me.

"Kinda snake-like." I wouldn't look her in the eye.

"Girl, what you talkin' 'bout? Snake-like."

I didn't want to tell her, and I wouldn't. "It doesn't matter, Mozell. Angel must have slipped on a log and fell over the waterfall and got killed. I don't know what else could have happened."

"Well, you was there. Did you see her fall?" She eased back on the swing.

"No. We got separated when I screamed, and that's when she must have hurt herself, but none of us knew it. And today, I took Charlie up to show him the waterfall, and there was Angel." I got quiet.

"Hmm. I see." Mozell squeezed my shoulder. "Well, child. You done seen most of it, and maybe there's more, but you got to deal wid your lie. It don't seem too bad to me."

"But maybe Angel would be okay if I had told people where we went for real."

"Maybe so, but seems to me Angel done got hurt when you weren't with her. Was you lookin' at her all the time while you was up there?"

"No."

"Well, den. You couldn't done nothin' to help her. You got to learn, Maggie. Sometimes God has plans we don't see."

"I don't understand."

"Is kinda like me and Joshua. I didn't see that train comin', and he didn't. You didn't see Angel, and whatever happened to her, she didn't see comin'. We jist got to go on. I got Joshua's tin to keep me company. You'll jist have to find somethin' to remind you of Angel. She's in your heart, jist like Joshua's in mine."

I reached in my pocket and rubbed the cross. I almost told Mozell about it, but I didn't. "She's in my heart."

"I know." Mozell shifted on the swing. "I's mighta stayed in Birmingham, but after Joshua was gone, I couldn't. So I moved here, in dis ol' slave shack my granddaddy used to live in. I came home, and I ain't never been sorry. Them mountains and that river is in my blood. I got friends here, and my chil'rens visits me, and I's most needs content."

I looked through the pines at the mountain. I loved it here too, but it was hard to imagine that it would ever be the same. "What should I do about my lie?"

"I specks you'll have to own up to it. You'll find a way. It don't sound that bad to me." She put the lid on the bread tin. "Take it back inside—'less you wants another."

"No, I'm done." I carried the tin into Mozell's cabin and placed it carefully on the table. She kept her place clean. The little panes in the windows were shiny, and the red and white curtains were starched stiff as boards. The other room was her bedroom, which held a small iron bed and one dresser. A rag rug lay at the foot of the bed, and an old wooden chair was next to the window. I could see the pine trees outside and the outhouse a ways away. I loved this place, and I loved Mozell.

"Girl. What y'all doin' in there? You done had time to put those cookies back a dozen times. You best get out here. I think I sees your brother comin'."

I jumped. Charlie coming here? He'd only been here once before, when I was late for supper. I didn't think I was late. I ran outside and looked up the road. Sure enough, it was Charlie.

"Maggie. Maggie!" He yelled. "You got to go home." He came into the yard, carrying his Daisy in his left hand.

"I'm not late. Mom said I had an hour."

"Hi, Mozell," he said.

"Hello, Mister Charlie. Maggie and me was jist talkin' an eatin' cookies. You want one?"

"No, thanks." He looked at me real serious like. "We got to go. Mom is worried about you."

"Well, good grief. Me and Mozell are okay. What's the big deal?"

He looked at Mozell. "I guess you know about Angel?"

"I does."

"Be careful, Mozell, because Mom just found out from Mrs. Albright that Angel didn't fall from the log, like we all thought." He looked at me and then back at Mozell. "Somebody choked her."

"Oh, my lordy. Lordy, lordy." Mozell stood up and grabbed me. I thought she was going to squeeze the life out of me.

"Mozell, let go," I said. "You're hugging me too tight."

"Oh, child. You go home, and you be careful. Lordy." Mozell pushed me towards the steps.

Charlie grabbed my hand. He said, "Be careful now, Mozell. You hear? There's somebody real bad out there."

Charlie fairly dragged me out of Mozell's yard. I yelled, "I love you, Mozell! Bye!"

"Bye, child. Bye. I's love you."

Charlie let go of my hand. He was walking so fast that I could hardly keep up.

"Slow down," I said.

"Dang, Maggie. This is real bad. Mrs. Albright is terrible upset. Mom went over to her house."

"Somebody choked her? Why? Why would anybody do that to Angel? She never hurt nobody."

"You're just too young. You don't know about bad people."

"Well, you're not that much older than me. I do too know about bad people."

"Not bad ones like this." He stomped ahead of me.

"What could be worse than choking somebody to death?"

"There's other things you don't know about. Now, just let it go. We got to get home."

We fairly ran past the stream, towards the highway. I thought about the water moccasins that might be basking in the sun, and the leeches that waited beneath the water for unsuspecting creatures. Somehow, they didn't scare me. But someone Charlie thought was worse than a strangler did worry me. I didn't know what had happened to Angel, but it must have been something real bad. The person who did it must be real bad. Worse than a witch.

CHAPTER 11

As Charlie and me made our way over the bridge and across the river road, I saw the Walking Man coming at a slow pace. He waved to me.

"Did you see that?" I asked.

"What?" Charlie asked.

"The Walking Man waved to me."

"That's no big deal."

"He's a little scary."

"Gosh, Maggie. You sound like Ida Mae. He hasn't done anything to you."

"Well, suppose he's the one that hurt Angel!"

"Don't go playing detective. Chief Dinsdale will take care of that." As we continued walking, Charlie added, "And I'll bet he wants to talk to you real soon."

That brought me back to my senses. I felt my face flush. "You want to see me get into trouble, don't you?"

"You're the one that made up stories. Not me."

"So what?" Now I was mad instead of scared.

"Just don't go making up more stuff. That's all."

I looked back as we continued walking up Main Street, but Wallis was nowhere to be seen. He sure could disappear real easy. I fingered the cross in my pocket. Charlie had gotten away from me, and I ran to catch up. "You won't tell about the cross, will you?"

"I forgot about it until you mentioned it." He thought on it." No, I won't tell."

We were in the middle of town now. A large amount of people walked along the street and milled about. It surprised me to see so many people in town. Some men were sitting on a bench in front of Sue Ann's grill, smoking and talking. As we passed, one of them pointed at me and said something I couldn't hear, but I knew it must be about Angel. Maybe they knew I had lied. My stomach churned.

"Is Mom mad at me, Charlie?"

"I don't think so. She just wanted you home, and she sent me, so you'd be safe."

"I can take care of myself, mister."

"Sometimes you can be so ignorant, it makes me mad." He switched his Daisy from his left hand into his right.

"Well, I can."

"You're just an innocent little girl. You don't know nothin' about bad people and how mean they can be."

"Well, I do too. I know that Buddy's dad is mean to him."

"I'm not talking about that kind of mean. There's all kinds of hatefulness."

"Like what?"

"Oh, Maggie. I don't have time to explain all of it to you. You'll find out about meanness as you go along."

"You don't know everything, Mister Smarty Pants."

"Well, I'm not talking about it anymore." With that, he fired off a shot at nothing in particular. The BB found its mark somewhere in a tree that lined Oak Street.

I looked up the street towards Angel's house. Five or six cars were parked under huge trees that lined the lawns. I knew they must have brought people who wanted to help Mr. and Mrs. Albright. I had no idea how I would ever get over the loss myself. I never knew anybody who had died. We hadn't even had a pet die.

I looked up at the clouds forming along the tops of the mountains. As the clouds moved in, the sunlight was shut off. A cool wind began to blow, and I could smell the coming rain.

"Hurry up, Maggie. It looks like we're headed for a thunderstorm."

We walked faster. As we started up Old Looney Mill Road, a clap of thunder rolled along the mountain and echoed up and down the hills. Large raindrops splattered the macadam, and the warm tar sent steam skyward. In a matter of moments, the rain came down in sheets, pushed in all directions by the whirling wind.

Charlie ran for home, clutching his Daisy close to his chest. I ran as fast as I could, but it was no use; I got drenched. We jumped the ditch and ran for the porch. The rain pounded on the tin roof. Tinker sat huddled up against the screen door, her fur wet. Charlie went inside.

I stayed on the porch and watched the lightning flash in the valley and listened to the thunder roll across the mountainsides. Tinker whined and whimpered. She was scared. I was too, but not from the lightning. That I could see and hear. I was scared of things that I couldn't see or hear. Charlie knew something I didn't know—something he thought I was too little to know. One day, when I grew up, I would know everything. That afternoon, I petted Tinker's wet fur and hugged her and thought of Angel. I pulled the cross from my pocket and studied it. Mozell was right. As long as I had something of Angel's, Angel would always be with me. It gave me comfort, and I decided I would never be scared of anything ever again. Except maybe snakes.

CHAPTER 12

It rained the next three days straight. Sometimes there was lightning and thunder, but mostly, it just rained. The river rose, and the water backed up and then flowed into the bottoms. I wondered how Mozell was doing, but Mom wouldn't let me go see her. In the rain, I really didn't want to go anyway.

Angel's funeral was on the fourth day after Charlie and me had found her. It rained that morning as we drove to the Valley Baptist Church. Dad was quiet, but Mom told me what to expect. "You'll get a chance to see Angel one last time," she said.

"I know."

"You be sure to pay your respects to Angel's mother."

"What do we say?" Charlie asked.

"Just tell her you're sorry for her loss. You don't need to say too much, or it will upset her. This is a real hard day for her and Mr. Albright."

"Will Ida Mae be there?" I asked.

"I don't know. She's just a little girl, and Angel was her special friend. She doesn't understand any of this. You might see her at the gathering afterwards."

"Okay, Mom."

I didn't know what else to say or ask, so I got quiet. Charlie was fidgeting with his collar and necktie. I had on a blue dress and some white socks and patent leather slippers. Mom had made me tie ribbons on the end of my pigtails. I felt silly, but Angel would have loved to see me all dressed up. I would have worn Mary Janes in her honor, but I didn't have any.

We drove through town. Deeter's store was dark. Even Sue Ann's grill was closed for Angel's funeral. We clattered across the bridge and went left on the highway for about a mile to the Baptist church, which sat in a meadow alongside the river. The parking lot was full of cars. People cramped together under umbrellas as they made their way to the church steps through mud and puddles.

"There's Mozell." Charlie said.

"Where?" I jerked my head around.

"Over yonder by that big tree."

Mozell was getting out of the big, black sedan her son Willie drove. Her daughter Maxine, who used to clean house for the Albrights and took care of Angel when she was little, was trying to get a black umbrella raised but was having trouble. Mozell fairly shouted, "Hurry up, Maxine, you lettin' the rain mess me all up." She straightened her black hat and smoothed her black dress. Maxine said something I couldn't hear. Willie waited patiently by the back of the car.

"Come on, Maggie. Get under the umbrella." Mom stood waiting for me. Dad and Charlie had already started for the church.

I jumped out. "Can I sit by Mozell, Mom?"

"You know she'll have to sit way in the back. Do you want to do that?"

"Yes."

"Well, come along."

We plodded through the wet grass and the red clay. My family didn't go to this church, but most folks in town did. Some Sundays, I had come here with Angel, but Brother Cross was too long-winded. And too loud. I liked the Methodist church better. But this was special, and I didn't care how long Brother Cross might talk. It was Angel's last day to be with us.

Brother Cross was greeting people at the top of the steps. His white hair and beard were misted with water. "Good morning, little miss," he said to me. He smiled broadly. His big hands were cupped together in a sort of prayer mode. Mrs. Cross was holding a bible in one hand and a big umbrella in the other.

"Morning." I noticed a coffee spatter on his white shirt. Maybe it was tobacco juice. Nobody walked around with their hands in a prayer mode except Brother Cross. Nobody. I looked at Mrs. Cross and said, "Good morning."

"You were Angel's special friend, weren't you?" she said.

"I guess so."

"Well, this is hard for everyone, especially due to circumstances." She fussed with the collar on her black dress.

Mom pulled me inside the church. "What'd she mean?" I asked.

"Never mind, Maggie."

I looked back at Mrs. Cross. She was looking at me and shaking her head slow like. Mozell and Maxine and Willie were coming up the steps. I heard Brother Cross say, "Now, you're welcome in our church, but you got to sit in the back. And if there aren't enough seats, you'll have to stand."

Mom whispered, "Do you want to see Angel?"

I looked to the front of the church. Mostly all I could see were mountains of yellow and white flowers. I knew Angel was there, and I was scared. The last time I saw her, she was all muddy. I didn't know what to expect. "I guess so. Will you go with me?"

"Of course."

The church was packed with people. I think everybody in town must have been there, even the ones who only ever went to the Valley Tavern or the other bars in town. Dad and Charlie were seated near the center, about halfway down the aisle. Beside them was Cotton with his uncle, Deputy Bob, and the deputy's wife and twin girls. As we moved along behind the line of people, I looked for Buddy and his family. I didn't see them, but I knew Buddy would be there. Nothing would keep him away from this, not even his dad.

The line inched along, and we moved closer to the casket. Ladies were blowing their noses and wiping their eyes. "Terrible," one woman said.

Another woman shook her head and sobbed out loud. Her husband muttered, "They should hang whoever done this."

I got more scared. I squeezed Mom's hand.

"Are you okay?" Mom asked.

"Can you see Angel, Mom? Does she look funny or something?"

"I can see her, Maggie. She looks fine. Real fine."

As we got closer, I could see better, but I still didn't have a good view of Angel. The white casket sat on a stand. Half of it was covered with red roses and a sign that read ALWAYS OUR ANGEL. I felt tears coming. I tried to shut them off, but it was no use. Mr. and Mrs. Albright stood next to the casket. Mom hugged Mrs. Albright. She looked awful. Her eyes were puffy, and she didn't smile. I thought about the cross, but I didn't want to give it up.

"Hello. I'm sorry," I said.

Mrs. Albright nodded.

"Hello, Maggie." Mr. Albright put his hand on my head. "If you want to see Angel better, stand on this stool." He pushed a wooden step towards the casket.

When I climbed up, I could see Angel's face real good. She looked like she was sleeping. Her hands were folded in a little prayer. Her hair was curly and just like I wanted to remember it: clean and shiny. A pink bow covered one side. She had on a beautiful white lace dress. I couldn't see her feet, but I guessed she was wearing Mary Janes. I studied her face hard. Then I noticed a blue mark around her neck and leaned closer for a better look.

"You can kiss her, if you want," Mr. Albright said.

I stood tall and looked him in the eye. "She won't know if I kiss her," I said. "But I will whisper in her ear. She'll hear what I have to say."

Mr. Albright's eyebrows moved in a funny way. I knew then that I wouldn't cry. Maybe I wouldn't cry ever again.

I bent down close and told her something I had always wanted to tell her. Then I made a promise. I know she heard me.

"I'm going back by Mozell, Mom." I looked at Mrs. Albright. "Will Ida Mae be here?"

"She'll be along in a while. When the service starts." She began crying again. Mr. Albright put his arm around her. Mom patted her hand.

As I moved up the aisle, I looked to see if Buddy had come, but I still couldn't find him. The last of the people crowded into the church and stood on both sides of the pews and along the back wall. Mozell, Maxine, and Willie were on the left, near the stairs to the choir balcony.

Mozell smiled when I took her hand. "Hi, Maxine. Hello, Willie," I said. They nodded their heads. Mozell hugged me, and I could smell the sweet musky scent of her body. It made me feel better.

The people got quiet, and Mrs. Turner, the church piano player, began playing *The Old Rugged Cross*. People stopped whispering. An angry-sounding voice came from outside. I knew it was Buddy's dad. Then a softer voice said, "Now, Alton, just be pleasant." It was Mrs. Toliver. "It's Buddy's friend."

Buddy come into the church from the outer room. His red hair was slicked down and parted on the side. He wore clean jeans, a red plaid shirt, and a blue necktie. He even had on shoes. I think my mouth dropped open. When he made eye contact, I could see tears. I gave him a serious look, so he wouldn't be embarrassed. He nodded and walked right straight down the center, towards Angel. I moved into the aisle to look after him.

When he got to the casket, he stopped for a short time. Then he stepped up on the stool and leaned over. I know he kissed her good-bye. *Damn.* I felt tears—his and mine. He came up the aisle with a defiant look on his face. I went back to Mozell and leaned against her.

Buddy's mom and dad and little sisters stood inside the chapel door. All at once, Mr. Toliver said, "What are niggers doin' in here?"

"Alton, hush," Mrs. Toliver said.

Buddy looked mortified. People turned to look at Mozell, Maxine, and Willie. I felt Mozell stiffen. I grabbed her hand. Mozell stood real quiet, but Maxine mumbled under her breath. Mozell whispered, "Be still, Maxine. We's here for a funeral, not fightin.'"

Brother Cross came into the chapel. He said, "Why don't you and the missus go to that side of the church, Alton?" Buddy and his family moved away from us. Mr. Toliver gave Mozell a mean look.

The choir started singing *Old Rugged Cross*, and everyone joined in. Up front, Brother Cross was talking quietly to Angel's mom and dad. Mr. Albright went to a door to the left of the altar. He disappeared for a few minutes, then came back carrying Ida Mae. He walked up to the casket, and Ida Mae reached out to touch Angel. A woman in front of us sobbed.

Brother Cross led Mrs. Albright up to the casket, and they stood there for a little while. Ida Mae had turned her head away from the casket and leaned it on Mr. Albright's shoulder. She looked out over the crowd. Brother Cross closed the casket, and Angel was gone. Just like that.

Mr. and Mrs. Albright and Ida Mae moved to the front pew. Brother Cross went up to the altar as the last words were sung:

> *I will cling to the old rugged cross*
> *and exchange it some day for a crown.*

I reached inside the pocket of my dress and fingered that cross for the millionth time.

CHAPTER 13

Brother Cross was long-winded as usual. Inside the church, it was real hot. The rain had made it sticky. People were trying to fan themselves with anything they could. I felt myself drifting off, but I couldn't without falling over. Mozell would nudge me, and I would wake up and catch a few words. I don't remember everything the preacher said, but some things stood out, like "loss of innocence" and "evil men." Mozell, Maxine, and Willie said "amen" to a lot of his preaching. Nobody else said much out loud.

Then he talked about Jesus and his forgiveness but said that some things were near impossible to forgive. A few people in front of us said "amen" to that. I think I might have even said it. It seemed like "amen" was catching.

Brother Cross kept talking, and people fanned themselves even harder. I felt sweaty.

In between his preaching, we sang *Rock of Ages* and my favorite, *In the Garden*. I loved to sing that song, and the words had special meaning for me now. When Mrs. Turner thumped the first chords, I got ready.

> *I come to the garden alone, while the dew is still on the roses,*
> *and the voice I hear whispering in my ear ...*

I looked up at the casket covered with red roses, surrounded by white and yellow flowers, and I knew that Angel would be in that garden. I sang real loud so she would hear.

All at once, a terrible clap of thunder shook the whole building. The lights flickered on and off, and Mrs. Turner stopped playing. The door to the left of the altar opened, and the Walking Man stood there in a plastic see-through raincoat. All he had on was his black crown hat, his black walking boots, and his underwear. Mozell called, "Lordy be, Wallis. Lordy be. Has you lost your mind?"

The Walking Man looked our way. A couple of women screamed. One fainted. Ida Mae shouted, "He's a witch! He's a witch! He killed Angel and threw her in a ditch!"

Wallis stood looking at us. It felt like time froze. Then another flash of lightning was followed by a rolling thunderclap. The Walking Man tipped his hat and shut the door. Ida Mae continued bawling, "He's a witch. He's a witch."

Deputy Bob got to his feet. Commotion filled the church. Buddy's dad yelled, "That's probably who kilt that little girl! We should hang 'im!" Some amens were shouted.

Chief Dinsdale and Deputy Bob went out the altar door. Brother Cross motioned for people to sit down. There was shuffling of feet and mumbling talk. Mom glanced back at me, then she and Dad sat down. Charlie looked at me and rolled his eyes.

It got real quiet.

In the silence, Mr. Toliver spoke out again. "That man is guilty as sin of harmin' that little girl. Who else in this town would do such a thing?"

Brother Cross fairly yelled, "This is no time to be going in that direction, Alton. Today is our town's special good-bye to Angel. Now, be quiet."

Mozell said soft like, "Amen." I did too.

There wasn't too much sermon after that. Brother Cross preached in the dark to a hot, sweaty group. The Walking Man had changed the mood. I didn't know what to think. Wallis was strange, but I wasn't ready to believe that he would hurt Angel. Of course, I couldn't believe that anyone would, but it had happened. Charlie was right. I didn't understand about some things.

Finally, Brother Cross had us all rise, and we recited "The Lord's Prayer." When the last "amen" was said, he moved from the altar. Then Mr. Albright and some other men lifted Angel's casket off the stand. They stood waiting behind the preacher while Mrs. Albright, Ida Mae, and some of their family and friends lined up behind the casket.

"What are they doing?" I asked Mozell.

"I specks they be takin' the child out to the cemetery. Her folks walks behind the casket. That's how it's done."

"When can we go?"

"They'll go by rows, honey. Now, you know that me and Willie and Maxine has to go last. You might want to go wid your folks."

"I want to be with you. Why do you have to go last?"

"Because that's the way it is."

Maxine spoke up. "Dumb, that's all. Shouldn't be like that. I knowed that girl better than most here."

"Be still, Maxine. I done told you that now twice. That's enough." Mozell said.

Maxine mumbled.

As the casket passed by, I could smell the roses. Some people carried the vases of yellow and white flowers. When Mrs. Albright passed, she saw Maxine and gave her a faint smile. The ladies in line wiped their eyes and blew their noses. The men looked mad.

It was slow getting out of the church, because there were so many people. It looked like a sea of black, inching its way to the door. I thought of the crow. I don't know why, but I did.

I was waiting with Mozell when Buddy got to the aisle. "You want to go with me?" he asked.

"I'm going with Mozell." I said.

"Go on wid your friend." Mozell pushed me towards him. "I'll be along."

I squeezed her hand and went with Buddy. I was glad that his mom and dad were ahead of us. I didn't want to walk with Mr. Toliver.

When we got to the door, I was happy to see it had stopped raining. The grass was still wet, and puddles were everywhere, but the sky had brightened. I hoped the sun would come out. Buddy and me were going down the steps when Cotton joined us.

"Makes me mad," he said.

"Me too," said Buddy. "We need to talk. I been thinkin' about that day and I just wonder if those men had anything to do with Angel."

I got scared. "You didn't say nothin' to anybody, did you?"

"I ain't said nothin' to nobody. My dad keeps askin' me where I was that day, and I keep tellin' him we were down by the river." Buddy wiped his nose with his hand.

"You can't ever tell your dad where you were, Buddy." I said.

"I keep thinkin' maybe I should. Maybe it would help."

Cotton said, "I been thinking that myself. Maybe we should tell. My uncle asks me almost every day about what Ida Mae said about the witch and the waterfall, and I just tell him we went that way once, but not the day Angel came up missin'."

"You better not tell. We made a promise. It isn't the right time."

"When will it be, Maggie? This has got away from us." Cotton kicked at a puddle.

We walked around the side of the church to the cemetery. Near the woods, there was a big, white tent with most of the people standing under it. As we got closer, Brother Cross said, "Get under the cover if you can. No tellin' about the rain. It might start up any minute."

"Promise me," I whispered. "Let's talk about this later. Nothing we do now will change anything. Promise?"

"Okay, Maggie," said Cotton.

"Buddy? Promise?" I pleaded.

Buddy had tears in his eyes. He sighed, then said, "I guess I can wait."

I hugged him. If he said anything, Buddy would get a terrible beating, and Mr. Toliver for sure would think the Walking Man had hurt Angel. I didn't want any of that to happen. On top of that, I had lied something fierce to a lot of people. I wouldn't be in a good place myself. And Cotton had lied to his uncle, Deputy Bob. I wished we had never found that waterfall.

We stood together at the edge of the tent. Water dripped off and hit me in the head. I moved, but it happened again. So I just thought about what Mozell had once told me, "Rain's jest God's tears." I had laughed at her, but now I thought maybe she was right. She and Maxine and Willie stood a ways off, near a big oak tree, looking our way. I waved, and she smiled.

Brother Cross asked us to bow our heads. Then he started talking about ashes and dust. People sobbed and cried. I held Buddy's hand on my right and Cotton's on my left. We stood that way through the whole good-bye. When I opened my eyes at the last "amen," the sun broke through the clouds. The trees and grass and flowers had never looked so full of color. It made me laugh, and it made me cry.

CHAPTER 14

After the graveside service was over, I hung around, waiting for the people to leave. Maxine walked right through the crowd to Mrs. Albright. They hugged. The other people hung back. Maxine turned away, and I saw tears streaking her face. She walked to where Mozell and Willie waited. I waved to them as they left.

When Mom and Dad had finished talking to the Albrights, they came over to me. "We're all going down to the church basement," Mom said. "There's to be a get-together. We'll have food and take time to be with the Albright family."

"I want to stay here for a while."

She lifted my face towards hers. "Are you all right?"

"Sure, Mom. I just have something I need to see."

Dad hugged me. Charlie gave me a weird look. "What do you need to see?"

"Never mind, Charlie. Just never mind."

He shrugged. I had to wait another ten minutes or more for all the people to leave the grave. Mrs. Albright looked at Angel's casket for a few minutes. Then she kissed it and patted the lid. Ida Mae clung to her dress. I could hardly bear to look at the little girl. I wondered if Ida would ever smile again.

Mr. Albright picked Ida Mae up. She leaned her head on his shoulder. The three of them left the casket and walked out into the sunlight. I hid behind a seeming mountain of flowers. I didn't want to talk to Mr. Albright again, and I didn't know what to say to Angel's mother. I was also afraid Ida would cry if she saw me.

When they were gone, I walked around the casket several times. I had never been this close to death before. A green carpet surrounded the entire area of the grave. The casket had been set on a table-like structure that was covered with the same green material. Looking down, I could see the hole below.

"If I could change it, Angel, I would. You know I would. And I will keep my promise."

I picked up some red clay and laid the lump on top of the white casket.

"Who you talkin' to?"

The voice startled me. It was Randal.

"Nobody." I swallowed hard. "I was just saying good-bye to my friend."

He looked at me hard like. "Yeah. That's why I'm here."

"I didn't know you knew Angel."

"Everybody knew Angel. She was sweet."

Another voice asked, "What's y'all doin'?"

I didn't see the man walk up, but he had a shovel. I took a sideways look at Randal.

"I'm just leavin'. I was saying good-bye. Angel was my friend."

"Y'all can stay, but I have work to do."

"I know. But, I'm leaving," I said.

"Me too," Randal said.

I ran out from under the tent and headed toward the church. I didn't look back. I don't know what happened to Randal, but he didn't come to the basement of the church, and I was glad.

My leather shoes clattered on the cement steps leading to the basement. The room was full of people sitting on fold-up wooden chairs around paper-covered tables. I could smell fried chicken, baked beans, and apple pie. The church ladies had made a huge meal for everyone. Mom had sent her famous chocolate cake, called a Million Dollar Cake, and I was determined to have some.

Buddy came up to me. His blue tie hung loose, and the top of his plaid shirt was unbuttoned. "Where you been?" he asked.

"I was just down by Angel."

"Oh."

"Randal was there, and he scared me," I said.

"He scares a lot of people, but I guess he's harmless."

"Who's harmless?" Cotton walked up, carrying a plate of food.

"Randal," I said. "I don't like him."

Cotton put a spoonful of baked beans in his mouth. "Uncle Bob says not to worry about Randal. The war just got to him. I think he was on some sort of beach, like Omaha or something."

"Ain't that in Nebraska?" Buddy asked.

Cotton laughed. "Well, yeah, but during the war with the Germans, they named a beach where they fought them after Omaha."

"What's that have to do with him acting so strange?" I asked.

"Beats me. Uncle Bob says it was real bad, and a lot of soldiers got killed and stuff like that. Maybe it made Randal goofy."

"Maybe. Anyway, he still scares me," I said.

Cotton said, "He might scare you, but I'm startin' to get scared about all the questions I'm being asked about where we played the day Angel came up missin'."

"Me too," said Buddy. "My dad is buggin' me all the time about it. He says he's about positive we weren't by the river."

"Look, Buddy. I know it's hard to keep lying, but I got my reasons. You have to trust me on this." I gave him my most pitiful look. "You promised."

"Gosh, Maggie. I don't get it. I know I promised, but it's real hard keeping a secret sometimes. I guess I can wait a little longer."

I smiled. "Let's get something to eat. Cotton's way ahead of us."

Cotton sat at an empty table, while Buddy and me got in line behind Mrs. Turner, the piano lady, and some of her choir members. The plates were stacked high with fried chicken, potato salad, baked beans, macaroni salad, rolls, and butter. One whole table held every kind of dessert. I passed by the puddings, the Jell-O, the

pies, and pink and white cakes and headed straight for the choco-
lates. I spied Mom's cake pan. *Damn.* It was empty. Nothing but
crumbs.

"Aren't you havin' dessert, Maggie?" Mrs. Turner asked.

"I don't guess I am."

"I made a nice apple pie. Right there it is." She pointed to a pie
that no one had touched. There wasn't one piece of crust missing.

"I believe I'll have a piece of white cake, thank you. I'm not par-
tial to pies."

"Suit yourself," she said.

I grabbed a hunk of the nearest white cake I could find. I had
made the mistake of eating a piece of Mrs. Turner's pie once before.
It looked like a lot of other people knew about her pie. I don't know
how they knew it was hers, but they knew.

Buddy whispered, "I can't stand her pie."

"Me either. Let's go sit by Cotton."

Cotton was almost finished eating. He had a big piece of Mom's
cake.

"Aren't you full?" I asked.

"No." He gulped down some iced tea.

"Don't you like white cake better than chocolate?"

"No."

"She's just trying to get your cake, Cotton," Buddy said as he sat
down.

"Be quiet, Buddy," I said. "I got my own cake."

Cotton laughed. "I know what she's doing." He took a big bite of
Mom's cake. "Mmm. This sure is good. I'd pay a million dollars for
this cake."

"I don't even care. I can have it any time I please." I took a bite of
chicken.

"I'd also pay a million dollars to know who killed Angel." Cotton
said soft like.

"You think them people that was shootin' at us might have done
it?" Buddy asked.

The basement was full of noisy, loud people, but when Buddy said that, I thought he had fairly shouted. I expected the crowd to stop what they were doing and look at us. I felt my face turn beet-red. "God almighty, Buddy. Don't talk so loud."

"Well, do you?" He tried to whisper.

"I don't know. I just don't know. I do know she wasn't shot."

Cotton licked chocolate off his fingers. "My uncle says she was choked."

I thought of the dark mark on her neck, but I didn't think the mark was big, like hands. It looked more like the size of Angel's necklace. "Are you sure?"

"I'm not sure about anything. I just know what Uncle Bob says. He knows more about it than I do." He sucked icing off his thumb.

"I still think them people that chased us might have had something to do with this." Buddy spooned some potato salad into his mouth.

"What about Wallis?" Cotton asked.

"I don't think he could do something like that," I said.

"Why not? We were following him, you know." He ate the last of the chocolate cake.

"Maybe we were, and maybe we weren't."

"What's that mean?" asked Cotton. "You said he went that way."

"I said I thought he did. Maybe he didn't."

"Well, this sure is a mystery," Buddy said. "I'd just like to kill whoever done it." He left for the dessert table.

I was stunned. He sounded like he meant it. "You think he could do that?" I asked Cotton.

Cotton was sucking on ice. "I reckon he could. He don't say much, but he's plenty mad. He was sweet on Angel."

"I know. I loved her too." I fussed with my white cake as my other hand touched the cross in my pocket. I glanced over to where Buddy was studying all the desserts. "If I tell you something, Cotton, you promise not to tell Buddy?"

He spit the ice back into his glass. "What?"

"Promise?"

"You better hurry. He's gonna come back." He stared at me. "I promise."

"I saw his dad up by the waterfall. That's part of why I screamed."

"No kiddin'?"

"And he was fooling around with a blond woman."

His eyes got big. He leaned in closer. "What else?"

"I'm not telling everything." I took a big bite of my white cake.

"Not telling everything about what?" Charlie sat down next to me.

"Me and Cotton were talking. This is none of your business."

"Well, you better finish up because we have to go. Dad's got some work to do, and I have to help him," Charlie said.

Buddy came back with two cups of vanilla pudding and a piece of cherry pie. "Hello, Charlie. Where you been? I haven't seen you for a while."

Charlie stood up and poked Buddy on the shoulder. "I just been around. Come on, Maggie. We have to go."

I glanced at Cotton. He would keep his promise, but I wasn't sure for how long. "I'll talk to you later."

Cotton winked at me.

"See you later, Maggie." Buddy dug into his pudding.

I dumped my paper plate into the trash barrel and took my flatware and glass to the kitchen window and placed them on the metal shelf. As I walked back by the dessert table, I noticed that Mrs. Turner's apple pie was still there.

At the steps, I took one last look at Buddy and Cotton. They were talking. I prayed Cotton would keep his promise.

Then I went up the steps and out into the warm sunlight.

CHAPTER 15

The drive back home seemed long. I stared out the window of the station wagon and looked at the bright-green mountains. The rain had made the leaves shiny, and even the pine trees seemed to glow. Patches of darkness drifted along the tops of the mountains as clouds moved across the sunlight. It made me think of all the summer days when us kids had played together. And I thought of Wallis. He acted crazy, but not that crazy. But what does a nine-year-old know? A lot of things. Maybe not enough. Would we ever play again? Could it ever be the same?

"Mom, can I go over to Mozell's?"

"What do you think, John?" Mom asked.

"I suppose it's okay." Dad made eye contact with me in the rearview mirror. "You shouldn't stay more than a few hours. I'll send Charlie for you when he finishes his work."

"I don't need Charlie coming for me. I can handle myself."

"Do you want to go or not?" Dad sounded sharp. I knew when to be quiet.

"I want to go. I'll wait for Charlie to come get me."

Charlie poked me in the leg. I slapped his hand.

We crossed the bridge into town. A lot of cars were parked near Sue Ann's grill. It was open now, and men milled around the sidewalk, leaned against the building front, sat on the benches, and squatted down on the sidewalk. They were all talking and smoking and spitting. Dad slowed to a crawl. "What do you suppose they're talking about?" asked Mom. "They look angry."

Dad cranked his head sideways. "I can't hear what they're saying, Laura. I'm sure it's about ... well, you know."

"About Angel?" I asked.

Both Mom and Dad answered at the same time, "Yes."

Just as we passed the grill, Chief Dinsdale and Deputy Bob came out of the brick police station at the center of town. Wallis was with them. He still had on his see-through raincoat, but now a T-shirt and some grey pants hung loose around his thin body. The chief and Deputy Bob were talking to him.

Someone yelled. "There he is, that son of a bitch!"

I turned to look out the back of the window, and Charlie did the same. The men down by Sue Ann's hollered and raised their fists in the air.

Chief Dinsdale yelled, "Be quiet, boys! I got no reason to jail Wallis. We're going over to Bryce Hospital in Tuscaloosa. After a few days, the doctors will tell us what's what. So just hold your horses." He ushered the Walking Man into the back seat of the police car. Deputy Bob got in front with Dinsdale.

When Dad turned onto Old Looney Mill Road, me and Charlie twisted around to face the front.

"He's taking him to the crazy house," I said.

Dad spoke. "Maggie, that's no way to talk."

"Well, that's where he's going, isn't it?"

"After what he did at the church, I can see why Chief Dinsdale wants to get the Walking Man checked out. I'm sure it's just a precaution." Dad sounded matter-of-fact.

"But Dad, Wallis didn't hurt nobody," I said.

"Chief Dinsdale is just making sure that he doesn't have some health problems," Dad said.

Charlie chimed in, "Or problems in his head."

"That's enough, Charlie." Mom turned back towards us. "We need to be kind. Others may not be as fortunate as we are. Now, don't worry about the Walking Man."

I couldn't let it go. "Well, I know he didn't hurt Angel. I know that's what people think. He said hello to me the other day, and I wasn't even scared."

Charlie poked me. He screwed up his face in an ugly way and mouthed: *Crazy.* I got mad, but I didn't say anything.

Nothing else was said. When we turned into our driveway, Tinker was sleeping on the porch. She jumped alert, barking a welcome and wagging her stubby tail. I forgot about being mad at Charlie. She made me smile.

I ran to the porch and hugged her. "I'm going to change my clothes and then go to Mozell's," I said to Dad.

"Okay, Maggie. Charlie is going to help me screen some small display signs for U.S. Steel, and then he'll be along after you."

"I'll take my Daisy," I said as Dad opened the front door. "I don't need Charlie to come for me."

I started to move past Dad, but he reached out to stop me. In a quiet voice, he said, "Now, Maggie, there is no discussion about this. Charlie will come for you." His look told me that it was final. He wasn't angry. Dad didn't get angry very often. In fact, he had never whipped Charlie or me.

I went to my room and shut the door. I took off my blue dress and hung it in the closet. I wouldn't wear it again all summer, unless I went to Sunday school. I didn't think I would, because I was mad at God. I stuck my good shoes into the closet. As I pulled on my jeans and striped cotton shirt, I remembered that the cross was still in the dress pocket. Just as I started to get it, there was a knock at my door. I ran to the bed.

"Maggie, it's Mom. I need to talk to you."

"Come on in." I began lacing up my Keds.

Mom came in and sat on the bed. "I know this is a hard time for you, but there's something I need to explain."

"You mean about Angel? I know there's something else, because Charlie and Cotton say stuff, but they don't tell me anything."

"Yes, it's about Angel." Mom fidgeted, and I knew it must be something serious, because usually she just said what was on her mind. "There were things done to Angel that were not nice."

"Like strangling her? I know."

"No, Maggie, not just that." She paused. "Whoever killed Angel touched her private parts in a mean way."

"You mean down there?"

"Yes." She took my hands in hers. "I know you don't understand, but in time, you will. You must be very careful about who you talk to. Whoever hurt Angel isn't right in their thinking."

"Is that why those men were so angry about Wallis?"

"Yes."

"Well, the Walking Man is strange, but I don't think he would hurt Angel. Heck, we follow him around all the time, and he hasn't hurt nobody."

"What do you mean, 'all the time'?"

Damn, I just about gave everything away, I thought. "I mean, sometimes we follow him. It's just a stupid game. It doesn't hurt nobody."

"Doesn't hurt *anybody*," she corrected me. "Well, if he comes back from Tuscaloosa, you children better stop following him until all this is settled." She touched my face. "There are people out there, Maggie, who hurt other people, including children. You need to be mindful. I'm not saying he's the one who hurt Angel, but right now, no one knows who did."

"Okay, Mom." I didn't know what else to say.

She got up and moved to the door. "You can go to Mozell's for a little while, but you have to wait for Charlie to come and get you."

"I will. I'll be safe, because I'm taking my BB gun."

She smiled. "That's probably a good idea."

After she left, I got the cross out of the dress pocket. I studied it for a few seconds and then stuffed it into my jeans. I grabbed my Red Ryder and a tube of BBs.

As I went out the front screen door, I vowed to practice target shooting every day. Then nobody could hurt me, not when I had my Daisy with me. I'd let 'em have it right between the eyes.

Tinker jumped up when the screen door slammed. I stopped for a few minutes to pet her. Her coal-black eyes studied my face, and then she licked my hand. I had everything a kid could want, except Angel.

CHAPTER 16

I decided to walk through town instead of taking the back way to the river. I don't know why. Maybe I was a little scared of meeting whoever had hurt Angel, but that was dumb, because nobody knew who hurt Angel. I wouldn't know the person if I saw him. It could be almost anybody in town. Heck, it might be Buddy's dad. He had been nearby, and I knew he could unzip his pants fast. Plus he was mean. I just couldn't be sure. A lot of people thought the Walking Man did it, but it didn't seem fair to me to think he was the one.

All kinds of crazy thoughts went through my mind as I walked down the macadam. Along the way, I shot at different targets, but I didn't hit anything. Charlie would have to give me some pointers, or I'd never be able to protect myself. Roy Rogers or even Dale could shoot the hairs off flies. If I practiced, I could be just as good. I stopped to shoot at a fence post. *Damn, missed again.* It was going to take time to get it right, and I felt like I needed to learn real quick.

As I came to the edge of town, a group of men came out of Sue Ann's. They milled around on the sidewalk in front of the café. A couple looked like the ones I had seen in the woods the day Angel disappeared. They were leaning on the backs of their Chevy pick-ups, smoking and talking.

When I got closer, I saw Buddy's dad in the group. A man in a white shirt with a black tie was talking to them. He had curly, brown hair and wore dark pants. I didn't know him, and I knew almost everyone in town. He looked at me as I passed. I looked away, but I heard Buddy's dad call him Mark. I remembered that Mark was the man the blond woman had talked about in the woods. Maybe he did it. I kept on walking towards the bridge and didn't look back. As I neared the middle, someone yelled.

"Hey, Maggie. Wait up!"

Buddy was on the river road, walking towards the bridge. He wore dirty jeans and a red pullover shirt, and his feet were bare. This was the Buddy I knew. I waited by the bridge rail. "What are you doin'?" I asked.

"Nothing. You goin' somewhere special?"

"No, not really. I was going to Mozell's. You want to come along?"

"I'll walk you over there. You shouldn't be wandering around by yourself." He threw a rock into the river.

"Now, Buddy. You know I can take care of myself."

He looked me straight in the eyes. "A few days ago, I believed we all were safe. I don't believe that no more. My dad is mean, Maggie, but whoever touched Angel is the meanest son of a bitch goin'."

"Buddy, don't you talk like that. Your mama would blister you."

"I don't care. It's true. I'd like to kill whoever done it."

He said it with so much hate that I was almost afraid. I had never seen Buddy look so fierce. "I know," I said, "but maybe the person who did it didn't mean to hurt her."

"You are just too kind." He threw another rock. It splashed with a clunky sound.

"I loved her too, Buddy, just like you did. But I couldn't kill the person. I couldn't do that at all." I began to walk away.

"Wait, Maggie. Let me go with you." He caught up to me. "Can I shoot your gun?"

"I reckon. You know how to shoot?"

"Let me have it, and I'll show you."

He took the Daisy and cocked the lever. He raised the Red Ryder to his right eye. "What are you going to hit?" I asked.

"See that pinecone yonder, in the tree on the other side of the river?" he asked.

"Which one? There's tons of 'em."

"Well, you just watch." He raised the Daisy slowly and took steady aim, then squeezed the trigger. A huge pinecone plopped into the river and floated away in the current. Buddy grinned. His red hair blazed in the sunshine. "How's that?" he asked.

"Dang. Teach me."

"I thought you was goin' to Mozell's." He squinted his blue eyes.

"Not anymore. I want to be able to shoot straight like that. Will you teach me?"

"You done asked me twice, so I guess I will. But you got to listen—and don't back-talk none." He handed me the Daisy.

"I'm not going to back-talk. This is serious."

"First off, we got to go into the woods, where there's all kinds of different stuff to shoot."

"What woods?"

"How about down where we followed the Walking Man?" Buddy asked.

"Down by the willow?"

"Yeah." He started back across the bridge.

"I'm kind of scared of those woods," I said.

"You don't need to be scared. I'll take care of you."

I followed him along the dirt road towards the willow. Buddy whistled as we walked along. I didn't want to be scared of the woods. We had played in them for a lot of summers. I knew I'd have to get over the feeling, and I sure didn't want Buddy to think I was afraid, so I started talking. "I saw your dad in town."

"I figured that was where he went."

"He was talking to some men. One of them had on some church clothes. You know, like a white shirt and a tie."

"Did he have curly hair?"

"Yeah."

We were by the willow tree now. Buddy stepped off the dirt road and went into the woods. "That's his boss."

I hesitated at the edge of the road. The pine forest looked dark, in spite of the sunlight. I looked closer. Shafts of light in the woods gave me courage. I gripped my BB gun tight and jumped the ditch. I was determined not to show any fear. "What's he do? I haven't ever seen him before."

"He sells stuff. Dad drives a truck for him, but he don't live around here. I think he lives in Birmingham."

"We go to Birmingham sometimes, but not often. Mom likes to shop at Loveman's or Pizitz, but I don't care if I shop there. I just like to eat lunch at Britling's. They have tons of food, and the macaroni and cheese is the best."

"I ain't never been to Birmingham, but when I grow up, I'll go. Maybe I'll get a job in the steel mill. I want to earn lots of money."

I handed him the BB gun. "Mozell's husband worked in a steel mill. She said it was hard."

"Can't be no harder than whackin' weeds and cuttin' wood or doin' a thousand other chores." Buddy took aim at some mistletoe high up in an oak tree. "Now watch this. You have to line your eye up with the sight on the front of the barrel and the slotted sight on the back."

I stood close to study how he was doing it.

"You have to be steady. No wobblin' around with your arms. Then you squeeze the trigger careful-like." He fired, and the mistletoe dropped to the ground. "See?"

"Let me try, Buddy. I know I can do it."

He handed me the gun. "Go over to that tree, and lean your arm against it to help you be steady."

"Well, you didn't do that."

"Remember what I said about arguing? Just do it, Maggie. Till you learn how to shoot real good."

I was a little indignant, but I did want to learn, so I did as he said. I leaned my right arm on a tree and sighted on a pinecone way up high. I lined up the front sight with the back one and squeezed the trigger. Bark flew, but the pinecone stayed where it was. "Dang it."

"You were a little high." He adjusted the rear sight. "Try it now."

I cocked the Daisy. I aimed again and took my time, trying to be steady. I fired. The bark to the right of the pinecone flew in all directions. "Are you sure you're telling me the right way to do this?" I was getting mad.

Buddy laughed.

"Don't you laugh at me."

"Well, gee whiz. You expect to hit the mark with only a couple of lessons? Just keep trying. Move the barrel a little to the left of where the last shot hit."

I tried again. I was real careful and real steady. *Bam.* The BB connected with the stem, and the pinecone dropped. "Hot damn!" I yelled.

"Hot damn." Buddy hugged me. "See? I told you. It just takes practice."

I was excited, because I had finally done what I wanted to do. It would still take a long time to learn how to shoot like Buddy or Charlie. We took turns shooting, and Buddy sometimes gave me pointers. I missed most things, but I did hit a few. The afternoon shadows lengthened as I poured the last of the BBs into the tube. While we were shooting again, we didn't hear the footsteps behind us.

"What's y'all doin'?"

There stood Randal. I know my face turned white.

"Golly, Randal." Buddy stood close to me. "You done scared us. What are you doin' out here?"

Randal's dark eyes looked us over. "I'm not doing anything. Just went for a walk, and I heard you laughing and shooting. You come here often?"

"No. Well, sometimes, maybe." Buddy shuffled his bare feet on the pine needles.

"You're a pretty good shot with that little rifle." He looked at me and smiled.

"Buddy's teaching me to shoot." I didn't like him calling my Daisy a little rifle, but I didn't say anything.

He stood looking at us. Smiling. I felt uncomfortable. I didn't know why.

"We better go, Maggie. We been here some time." Buddy started back to the road. I followed him, fast. Randal didn't say anything.

When we got out of the woods, I saw Charlie walking towards the bridge. "Hey, Charlie!" I yelled. "I'm down here with Buddy!"

Charlie stopped. He turned towards us and waited.

Buddy said, "Randal sure can sneak up on ya, can't he?"

"Gives me the creeps." I said.

"Me, too," Buddy agreed.

When we got closer to Charlie, I saw that he was carrying his Daisy.

"Thought you were going to Mozell's. It's a good thing I didn't walk all that way and not find you there. I've a good mind to tell Dad."

"Well, you didn't walk all that way, so you don't need to tell," I said.

"You're not supposed to go just running around wherever you please, you know."

"Who says, Mister Smarty Pants?"

Buddy laughed. "You sure got a fightin' sister."

Charlie rolled his eyes. "You just don't get it. It's changed now. Everything's changed."

I said, "I do get it, but I'm not letting some ol' crazy person scare me from doing what I want to do. Besides, I can protect myself." I patted my Daisy.

"Well, you can't protect yourself if you can't hit nothing," Charlie said.

"You want to challenge me to a shoot?"

Charlie leaned on the bridge rail. "See that pinecone on the second tree closest to the river? First one shoots it off is the winner. I go first."

"You're cheating, Charlie. Why should you go first? You know you'll knock it off and I won't even get a shot."

"Okay, you go first. It won't make any difference. I'll still win."

I'd show him. I leaned on the bridge rail and took a steady aim. I lined up the sight real careful and squeezed the trigger. The BB whizzed away and the bark flew. "Damn."

Charlie stood square in the middle of the plank bridge road and took aim. He fired. The pinecone sailed to earth. "Might as well go home," he said. "I'm the Grand Exalted again. Bye, Buddy." Charlie started towards town.

I was mad as hell.

Buddy said, "See ya, Charlie." Then he said to me, "You were close. Just keep practicing. You'll beat him one day."

I loved Buddy for that. Of course, I didn't love him as much as I had loved Angel, but I loved him. "Bye, Buddy. Thanks." I left him standing on the bridge.

I ran after Charlie. We walked in silence through town. Although some men were outside the Valley Tavern, most were still milling around Sue Ann's. I looked for the man in the white shirt, but he was gone. So was Buddy's dad. When we got home, Mom had dinner ready.

"How's Mozell?" Dad asked.

"Fine," I said.

Charlie kicked me lightly under the table, but he didn't say anything. He didn't have to. He was the Grand Exalted.

CHAPTER 17

The following morning, I was awakened by a cardinal singing in the magnolia bush outside my bedroom window. The sun had barely risen over the hill behind our house, but already it was hot. My forehead felt wet and sticky. I could hear Mom moving around in the kitchen. I walked out just as she was clearing the table.

"Where is everybody? What time is it?"

"Well, aren't you full of questions this morning? Good morning, Maggie."

"Morning, Mom."

"Your Dad and Charlie went fishing up on Lake Purdy. They'll be gone all day." She washed a plate and stacked it in the metal drainer. "It's about seven-thirty. Why are you up? I thought you'd sleep a little longer."

"It's hot. Some dumb ol' bird woke me up.

"Now, I know you don't mean that."

"It was real loud."

"Could it be the Bird of Jealousy?" She turned from the sink and looked at me. She had me. I managed to grin. "Would you like some eggs?"

"Yes. Well, they could have asked me to go."

"Charlie's been helping your dad quite a bit. It's his special treat. Now, go get dressed, and I'll fix your eggs and toast."

"Are there chores to do?"

"It's Saturday. Time to shake the rugs and dust."

I'd rather be fishing than shaking rugs, but I didn't say so. "Okay, Mom." I went to my bedroom and pulled the sheet up snug. The white bedspread was in a heap on the floor. I moved slow like. I didn't feel like making my bed.

Mom called, "Maggie, your breakfast will be done real soon. Get a move on."

Her voice snapped me into motion. I quickly took off my pajamas and put them under my pillow and pulled the bedspread tight. At least the bed was made—not real good but it was made. I grabbed underwear out of the dresser and put on my clothes. Even though it was hot, I would wear jeans. I always did. I hated the briars in the fields, and I thought my legs looked skinny. I looked at myself in the mirror, and my braids were a mess.

"Breakfast is on the table," Mom said.

I went to the kitchen and sat down. Mom was at the table, drinking a cup of coffee. "Can I have some?" I asked.

She eyed me for a moment. "I suppose so. But you'll have to have milk with it. You're too young for black coffee."

"Dang, I'm too young for almost everything! Knowing about Angel, drinking black coffee, having a BB gun. Being able to go by myself anywhere I want." I dipped my toast in my egg yolk.

Mom set a cup on the table and poured coffee for me. "Sounds like a hard life. Except you do have a BB gun, and you do go about where you want." She didn't pour milk into the coffee. Instead, she sat down and began drinking her own.

I poured ketchup on my eggs. "Can I try it black?"

"Go ahead. Suit yourself."

I took a big gulp. It was bitter as hell. I know I made a face, but Mom didn't say anything. "Maybe I'll put a little milk in it. It's kind of hot."

She handed me the milk. "What do you want to know about Angel?"

"I don't know, Mom. It's just that everybody says something nasty happened to her, and I don't understand. You told me about her being touched, but it seems like there's more."

She sighed. "You remember when you asked me about how babies are made?"

"Yeah."

"Well, honey, whoever killed Angel did that to her."

"You mean stuck his thing in her?" I was mortified.

"Yes. He put his penis in her."

"Why would someone do that? She was too little. She didn't love anybody like that."

"That's the point, Maggie. It was not a loving thing. This person is sick in the head, and it must be someone who lives here. Someone Angel knew who saw her by the river while you were playing."

"But we weren't—!" I stopped just in time. That lie was getting harder to keep. "But we weren't there that long, and I didn't see anybody except Cotton, Buddy, and Ida Mae."

"You said she left to change her shoes. So you didn't see her all the time."

I thought back to that day. Buddy's dad was so quick with slinging his thing around. It couldn't be. Maybe it was. I didn't want to think he would do it, even though I didn't like Mr. Toliver. "No, we didn't see her all the time." I sipped my milk coffee.

"You see now why Dad and I don't want you walking all over without us knowing where you are or who you're with. You see that, don't you?"

"I guess I do, Mom. It could be almost anybody, couldn't it?"

"Yes, it could." She finished her coffee. "You need to fix your hair. Then we'll do the dusting and the rugs. That won't take long."

"After we get done, can I go see Ida Mae?"

"I don't mind, but I'd better call Mrs. Albright to make sure it's okay for you to go."

I finished my eggs and toast and carried my dishes to the sink. There sure was a lot to think about. "I'll comb my hair. Will you braid it for me?"

"Well, you haven't wanted me to do that for a long time. Of course I will."

I went into my bedroom to get my comb and brush. The bedspread was not real smooth. I fixed it so that Mom would be proud, if she looked in. When I went back to the kitchen, Mom was saying her good-byes to Mrs. Albright. "She thinks it might be a good idea for you to visit with Ida Mae. The poor thing is taking it quite hard. You'll need to be thoughtful about what you say."

"I know."

I sat down and brushed my hair while Mom finished the dishes.

Once they were done, she took the brush and untangled the waves the tight braids had made in my hair. She brushed real slow. I had forgotten how nice it felt to have her do my hair. Sometimes it was better to forget about growing up so fast and wanting to do everything yourself. She took the comb and parted my hair down the middle, then separated one side into three strands and plaited my waist-length brown hair into a perfect braid. When I heard the second rubber band snap onto the other braid, I knew she was done.

"Let me see how you look." She placed her hands on my shoulders and spun me around. "Picture-perfect." She straightened the collar on my plaid shirt and smiled.

I hugged her. We stood that way for several moments. "Thanks, Mom."

"Thank you, Maggie."

I don't why she said that. It seemed strange, because I hadn't done anything. Somehow, I knew it was for many reasons that only she understood. Maybe I didn't know everything, and maybe I never would. But I was learning.

I smiled up at her. "Let's get our chores done, so I can go see Ida Mae."

CHAPTER 18

Soon after I snapped out the last of the throw rugs, I grabbed my Daisy and headed out the screen door. I gave Tinker a quick pat and ran across the yard, jumped the ditch, and landed on the macadam. The sun had risen higher. The tar oozed between the loose gravel. It was going to be a real scorcher. I had promised Mom not to wander around alone. She didn't have to worry. I'd shoot anybody who tried to do to me what he had done to Angel. And I knew right where I'd shoot.

I stopped several times along the way to the Albright house and shot at trees and fence posts. Sometimes I hit close to the mark, and sometimes the BB went wherever it wanted. I needed a lot more practice.

When I got close to town, I could see people outside of Sue Ann's. As I got near Oak Street, I stopped on the main road and stared. I could see Randal and Deputy Bob, and I thought I spotted Mr. Toliver's red head, but the others were just a blur. I turned up Oak Street and headed for the familiar white house.

I was a little scared. The house looked the same—same fence, same roses, same green shutters, same oak trees—but for some reason, it looked different. A black wreath hung on the front door. I had never seen one before, but I thought I knew what it meant. It reminded me of a black hole, and that was how I felt when I thought of Angel. Like a black hole was in my heart.

As I walked up the front steps, the door opened. Ida Mae stood there in a pretty little pink dress. "Hi, Maggie." She grinned.

She ran out to wrap her arms around me. I pulled her to me and hugged her for all I was worth. "Hello, Ida."

"Y'all want to come in?" Mrs. Albright stood at the door.

"Hello, ma'am. We can do what Ida wants to do, if it's okay with you."

"I want to go for a walk. I haven't been for a walk forever." She let go of me and turned to her mother. "Please? Can I go for a walk with Maggie?"

Mrs. Albright smiled at Ida Mae. She kind of pinched her lips together and then smiled again. "Yes. But you must promise to stay close to Maggie."

Ida giggled. "I will."

Mrs. Albright looked at me. "Y'all can go downtown, but don't go anywhere else." She handed me two dimes. "Take Ida to Deeter's. She might want some candy or some ice cream, and there's enough for you both."

I put the money in my jeans pocket. They clinked against the cross. "Thank you, Mrs. Albright. I'll take good care of Ida Mae. I won't let her out of my sight."

"I know you won't. Now, run along, but don't be gone too long. Hear?"

"Yes, ma'am." I switched my Daisy to my left hand and took Ida's hand in my right. I was glad Mrs. Albright had not asked about the waterfall and following the Walking Man.

We headed towards town. Ida fairly skipped and danced. I had to let go of her hand. She grinned and giggled. "Where's Buddy and Cotton?" she asked.

"I don't know, Ida. I suppose they're at home doing chores or something. Why?"

"Will we go looking for the Walking Man?"

"No, not today." I thought it strange that she would ask, but I didn't know how five-year-olds thought, so maybe it wasn't strange. "Aren't you afraid of him?"

"He made her an angel. A real angel."

"I know. But I'm not sure he did it, Ida."

"He's a witch."

I knew that nothing I said would change her mind, so I didn't try.

By then, we were at the edge of town. A lot of people stood along the streets, visiting with each other. Even though it was Saturday, there seemed to be more people than I remember ever being in town, except when we had a Fourth of July parade. Way down the street, I could see parents letting their kids off in front of the theater. The marquee listed an Abbott and Costello movie along with a Roy Roger movie. I wished I had asked Mrs. Albright if we could go to the movies, but I had forgotten all about Saturdays and matinees. It felt as though weeks had passed since Angel had gone missing and been found and then buried.

As we walked past the Mobile Savings and Loan where Mr. Albright worked, the people on the sidewalk stopped talking and stared at us. Some women whispered about Ida Mae and Angel, but they weren't loud, and Ida didn't seem to hear. I was glad. I wondered if Mr. Albright was working that morning. I supposed he would be. Deeter's General Store seemed miles away, but we finally got there.

The minute we walked inside, Deeter said, "Well, hello, girls. How are you today?" Tobacco juice slipped down the side of his mouth. He wiped it with the back of his hand.

"Hi, Mr. Deeter," Ida Mae said, then went directly to the candy case.

A few people were inside. A woman was looking at blouses towards the back of the store. A small child clung to her yellow sundress. Several men were over by the gun racks and cases, studying the rifles and handguns. They pointed the weapons toward the front windows at imaginary targets.

Ida Mae pressed her face against the glass case and moved slowly along it, eyeing every piece of candy. Her fingerprints and nose prints blended with all the other finger and lip and nose prints left there by other children. Some of them might have been mine, because I don't think Deeter washed the glass too often. I had already decided to buy five pinwheels and a single-dip ice cream cone.

As I waited for Ida Mae to decide, one of the men said, "Say, Deeter, I heard you got in a new revolver. A Colt."

"I did. But I'm waitin' to see if Deputy Bob wants it." He spit tobacco juice into a cup.

"Well, can I look at it?"

"Take a look. It's on the second shelf," Deeter said.

"Hell, I don't see it." The skinny man looked intently at the case.

Deeter moved from behind the cash register counter. "Are you blind, Earl?"

"I can see. It ain't there."

The other man laughed. Deeter moved behind the gun case and slid the door open. He got a funny look on his face. "Damn! God-damn."

The woman stopped looking at the blouses and covered the child's ears. "Mr. Deeter! I got a child here."

His face went beet-red. "I'm sorry, ma'am." He pushed doors open on other cases and rummaged around.

"What'd you do? Hide it?" Earl asked.

Deeter whispered, but I heard him. "Hell, no. It's plumb gone. Somebody stole it. Damn."

"Well, ain't that somethin'?" the other man said.

Deeter moved from behind the counter and yelled, "Randal! Come out here!"

Randal popped through the curtained doorway of the storage room. "What's wrong?"

"You sell that Colt?"

"No. Why?"

"Because it ain't where it's supposed to be." Deeter was clearly mad.

Ida Mae said, "I want two pinwheels and three caramels."

"Hush, now, Ida," I whispered. "Mr. Deeter is busy."

The men went to the front door. Earl spoke. "We'll see you later, Deeter. You got a lot on your mind." They left, mumbling to each other.

The angry look left Deeter's face as he looked down at Ida. "You got 'em, little girl." He got behind the candy case and pulled out a paper sack. "What do you want, Maggie?"

"I'm going to have five pinwheels and an ice cream cone. Ida wants ice cream too."

Randal came up by us. "You want anything else, Deeter?"

"No. Just go finish unpacking the can goods." Deeter motioned Randal away.

"I don't think Deputy Bob wanted the Colt, Mr. Deeter. Still, I'm sorry about your loss," I offered.

Deeter didn't say anything. He gave us our bags, then moved to the ice cream case. Ida stuffed a caramel in her mouth as she tried to see every color of ice cream.

"What're you going to have?" Deeter asked.

Ida didn't answer.

"I'll have butter pecan," I said.

He smiled at me. "I wasn't asking you. I know what you'll have. You always have that." He dipped a big scoop of butter pecan onto a cone and handed it to me.

"I'm going to have strawberry." Ida grinned.

He swirled the metal scoop in a glass of milky water and dipped up a scoop for Ida Mae. He wrapped a paper napkin around it. "You want some more napkins?" he asked me.

"Yeah, I guess that would be a good idea." I took them and stuffed them into my pocket. "I almost forgot. I need two packs of BBs."

He moved up to the front. On the shelves behind the register were lines of shotgun shells, bullets, and rows of BBs. He handed me two blue and white tubes. "You been shootin' some?"

"Practicing, mostly. How much do I owe you?"

He looked at us a moment. "Your candy and ice cream comes to twenty cents. The BBs will be another nickel a piece. That'll be thirty, young lady." He spit juice into a cup, which he set on the counter.

When I pulled the money from my jeans pocket, the cross came out too. I jammed my hand back into my jeans and worked it around until I felt one dime. I put that in Deeter's hand, then dug down for the other. He caught the second dime in his outstretched hand. "I got some nickels in my shirt pocket, Mr. Deeter."

"You got money all over yourself. How come you got so much?"

I knew he was kidding me. "I work hard, just like you do." I laid the nickels on the counter.

"Can we go now?" Ida asked.

I put the tubes of BBs in the left pocket of my jeans, along with the napkins. I licked the melting butter pecan from my cone. "Sure, Ida. Stay close to me. Maybe we'll go sit down by the river for a while." We headed out, with me juggling my Daisy in one hand and my cone in the other. "Bye, Deeter."

"Bye, girls. Be careful, hear?" He walked us to the screen door.

"We will."

Ida Mae walked real slow, licking melting strawberry ice cream carefully from the edge of the cone. I should have known I wouldn't need napkins for her. She was like Angel in some ways. She could get dirty, but not too dirty, and she didn't like to spill things on her dresses.

By the time we got down by the movie house, everybody was inside. Only a few kids were in the lobby, getting cokes and popcorn. I loved how the lobby smelled. The movie poster was *Abbott and Costello Meet Frankenstein,* which I'd seen twice already, so I didn't feel bad about not seeing it again. A couple of the kids ran over to the glass doors and stared at us. It made me sort of mad. Like we were freaks or something.

Ida Mae didn't seem to notice. She happily licked her ice cream and crunched the vanilla cone.

"You want a napkin?" I asked.

"No. I'm not dirty."

"How about your hands?"

She pushed the remainder of the cone in her mouth and inspected her fingers. They had some strawberry stains, so she stuck them in her mouth and sucked them clean. I laughed.

"Why are you laughing at me?"

"I'm not laughing at you, Ida. I just like how you clean your fingers." I popped my cone in my mouth and ran my tongue over my fingers. "See? I do it too."

She giggled and took my hand as we walked towards the river. Near the right side of the bridge, down a slight bank, someone had built a wooden bench under a tall oak. Ida Mae and me walked down to sit on the bench. The river flowed real slow under the bridge, and in its shadow, a large school of mullets worked the bottom. "See the fish, Ida?"

She stood to look in the direction where my finger pointed. "I see them. I see them! We should show Angel." She turned to face me. She was smiling.

I was stunned. "How are we going to show Angel the fish?"

"We'll just tell her where they are. She'll see them."

"But Angel isn't here, Ida. She's in heaven."

"I know that, silly. But God sees everything, and now Angel will too." She turned to look at the fish again.

I had to look away. I pulled a napkin out of my jeans and pushed it across my nose, then jammed the wet thing back in my pocket. "I think you're right, Ida. She can see them."

Ida looked at the sky and said, "Look under the bridge, Angel. See the fish?"

I looked at the white clouds drifting across the blue sky.

Ida sat back down and leaned against me. "I miss her, but she's happy. Mama said so."

"I miss her too, Ida. I miss her awful, but I know she's happy."

"Will you play with me sometimes, like Angel did?"

"Sure, I will."

She took my hand. "I love you, Maggie, but not as much as I love Angel."

"I know. I love you, Ida Mae, and I always will. You can count on that."

We sat on the bench for what seemed a long time, talking about Angel and the things she liked and the things she had done. Ida Mae was quite talky. She giggled and laughed and pointed at fish and birds and squirrels. I had worried about what to say to this little five-year-old girl, but she seemed older and smarter than my nine years.

Charlie was right again. I didn't know everything. Maybe never would.

CHAPTER 19

After we came back home from church that Sunday, Dad prepared the barbeque pit for our every-summer-Sunday picnic. Mom had already made macaroni salad, chocolate cake, and pickled eggs. The smell of baked beans cooking in the oven made me happy. Tinker ran around the kitchen, trying to keep from being stepped on. I was busy getting paper plates, napkins, and silverware ready to take outside.

Mom stood at the kitchen counter, making a salad. "Put Tinker out. She's getting in the way."

Tinker stared at me and wagged her stubby tail wildly. "There's nothing to eat yet, girl. You have to go outside. Come on," I said to her.

Tinker followed me until she figured where we were headed. I had to drag her outside. She took up a position in front of the screen door, just staring at me. *Dogs.*

I walked back to the kitchen. "Can I ask Buddy to come to our picnic?"

"I suppose so. We should have enough food." She sliced green bell pepper into the salad. "You know they don't have a phone. You'll have to walk down and get him."

"I know." I picked up all the paper plates and other things and started for the door.

"Tell Charlie to go with you!" she called.

I went back to the kitchen. "Do I have to?"

Mom turned from the counter. "Yes, Maggie, you do. I know it's hard, but until this thing is settled, I'd just feel better if you didn't wander around alone."

I felt like a little kid, but I wasn't going to argue with Mom. It wouldn't do any good anyway. I stomped through the living room and pushed the screen door open and banged Tinker's nose. She yipped. "Get out of the way, dumb dog."

Tinker followed after me, wagging her tail. I walked down the hill towards the apple trees, where Dad was basting chicken halves over the barbeque pit. Charlie sat next to him, drinking a bottle of RC. I set everything on the wooden picnic table I had helped build.

"Can I have an RC?"

"Sure." Dad said. "You been helping Mom?"

"Yes." I dug around in the ice-filled metal washtub for a bottle of RC. Charlie handed me the opener. "I'm going down to get Buddy. Mom said I could ask him to our picnic."

Dad smiled. "That'll be fine, Maggie. I like Buddy. I can't take you, though. I have to mind the chicken."

"I know. Mom says Charlie should go with me."

Charlie screwed up his face. "Why? I want to sit here."

"She said so. It wasn't my idea."

"Just go, Charlie. You know why." Dad brushed barbeque sauce on the chicken.

Charlie gulped down the rest of his RC. Tinker stood by him, wagging her tail. "Get out of my way, dumb dog."

"Don't talk to her that way," I said. "She's a nice dog. She loves you."

Charlie gave me a mean look. "C'mon. Let's go."

I patted Tinker's head.

Charlie had already started down the hill, so I ran to catch up. My RC sloshed around in the bottle. The fizz bubbled up, and when I took a drink, it made me sneeze.

"Stop walking so fast, Charlie. We're not in a race."

He slowed down. "Golly, Maggie. Am I gonna have to follow you around the rest of my life?"

"I don't like it either, but Mom is afraid that whoever killed Angel will hurt somebody else, and she doesn't want it to be me."

"Who'd bother you? Heck, they'd be afraid to."

We were at the bottom of Old Looney Mill Road, and I could see Main Street. "Maybe that's true," I said. "But look at all the people in town. It could be any one of them. Might be a big ol' scary man, or somebody we trust. I wish I knew who did it."

"You scared?" Charlie asked.

"Sometimes at night, I am. But mostly, I'm not."

"If you were to guess who did it, who'd you say?"

"I don't have any idea. Maybe one of those men who chased us. Maybe Buddy's daddy."

We passed Oak Street and reached Main. Bunches of people stood here and there, but they were mostly near the small jailhouse and Sue Ann's. "Why would you think Buddy's dad did it?" Charlie asked.

"'Cause he's mean to Buddy. Let's walk over on Deeter's side of the street. Those people look mad." I clutched my RC bottle tightly.

Charlie looked at the people. "You're right. They do look mad."

Just then, Chief Dinsdale drove up and parked in front of the jail. Charlie and me stopped in front of Deeter's to watch. Dinsdale got out of the car, and the Walking Man and Deputy Bob got out on the other side. Everyone's voices got loud. I heard words here and there: "Crazy." "He done it." "Hang 'im."

Deeter came out to the sidewalk with Randal. "What's goin' on?" Deeter asked.

"Looks like the Walking Man is back." Charlie said.

Deeter spit tobacco juice into the gutter. "Well, so he is. I reckon that'll get things stirred up again."

"What do you mean, Deeter?" I asked.

"Some folks think he's the one that done it."

"I'll bet he did," Randal said.

"I don't think he did it at all. He never hurt nobody." I eyed Randal and took the last drink of my RC.

"He's crazy," Randal said. "Walks around in black like some sort of old cowboy wandering all over the county."

I wanted to say that at least he didn't paint his car a different color every other week, but I didn't. Besides, Wallis didn't even have a car. "Just because he's different doesn't mean he did it," was the best I could do.

We stood there for a while. Chief Dinsdale led the Walking Man into the jailhouse. Some of the men shook their fists and yelled. Women pulled at the men to get them to leave. It made me nervous.

Deeter said, "C'mon, Randal. Back to work. There's nothin' to see."

"Will you take this empty bottle, Deeter?" I asked.

"Sure thing. I owe you two cents." He took the bottle and went inside.

Randal said, "He done it. I bet he done it." Then the screen door slammed shut.

"Let's go get Buddy, Maggie." Charlie moved down the sidewalk.

I looked back towards the jail. The door was shut, and most of the people had left. "Wait up, Charlie. I'm coming."

The Saturday afternoon matinee poster was gone. The Sunday night movie was *All About Eve*. Mom liked Bette Davis, but we were having a picnic, so she and Dad wouldn't go. I walked by a repair shop that had a television in the window. "You wish we had a television?" I asked Charlie.

"Sure, but it wouldn't do us any good. The reception is awful. Too many mountains. Someday I'll have one, maybe two. When I grow up and move away."

"What would you do with two? That makes no sense," I said.

"There might be a lot of different stations, just like the radio. Then I could look at baseball and a John Wayne movie at the same time."

"They won't have movies on television." I said it like it was true.

"They might. It doesn't matter, anyway. We don't have one."

As we walked by the Valley Tavern, a mixture of beer and barbequed pork smells came from inside the small brick building. Dad had painted the sign hanging over the doorway. I had gone with him to help hang it, and we had eaten barbeque sandwiches afterward. I loved the food, but I remembered the place as being dark. I tried to look through the window. It was still dark.

"Doesn't the barbeque smell good?" I asked.

"Yes, it does, and I'll bet ours does too. Now, hurry up. I want to get back home. I'm hungry."

Sometimes Charlie could be so aggravating. He didn't talk much, and he was always telling me to hurry up. I couldn't help it that my legs were short and his were long. We reached the bridge and turned left, towards Buddy's house.

When we got there, Buddy was sitting on the steps, swatting flies with a piece of rubber tire. He grinned when he saw us. "Hey. What y'all doin'?"

"We came to see if you could come to our house for a picnic. We're having barbequed chicken," I said.

He jumped to his feet. "Mom. Mom? Maggie and Charlie want me to come to their house for a picnic."

Mrs. Toliver came to the door, carrying the small child on her hip. Buddy's other sister clung to her faded dress. She smiled at us. "You can go, Buddy, but be home before dark. Now mind. You know how your dad gets. He might work tonight, and he might not, so you best be here before he gets back."

"Hi, Mrs. Toliver." I said.

"Hello, Maggie. How are y'all?"

"Fine."

Charlie waved a little wave as he headed out to the road. Buddy walked beside him. I was thankful that no snakes had come out from under the house. "Bye," I called back.

"I sure am glad you came to get me," Buddy said. "I didn't have nothin' to do, and I didn't want to go fishin'."

"Dad and I went fishing yesterday up to Lake Purdy," Charlie said.

"You catch anything?"

"Not much. It's too hot, and all the rain made the mosquitoes thick, so the fish had plenty to eat."

"Yeah. I kinda thought that might be a problem." Buddy said.

I secretly smirked.

We were quiet for a while. It was quiet all around, until we got to town.

The people must have come back and brought others with them, because the town was full of people. Mostly, they were hanging around the jailhouse. Sue Ann had opened her café, and people wandered in and out with drinks and bags of potato chips.

"What's goin' on?" Buddy asked.

"They brought Wallis back," I said.

"Well, dang. It looks like a party or somethin'." Buddy slowed down to look. "The Walking Man ain't that special, is he?"

"He's getting more special every day," my brother said.

"Well, heck. Who we goin' to follow if everybody's watchin' him?"

"They think he killed Angel." I said.

Buddy stopped in front of the jail. "Folks in this town are dumb. Wallis has lived here all his life, and he's always been weird. Why would he just up and kill somebody now? It don't make sense. What do you think, Charlie?"

"I don't know. I don't know much about why people do anything they do. But somebody in this town did it. They had to know about the waterfall."

"Hush, Charlie," I said. "You want folks hearing?"

"Well, they know where she was found. It doesn't mean they know you and Buddy and Cotton were there when she was." He walked away.

"Hey, Maggie!" someone yelled. I looked down towards Deeter's. Cotton was walking toward us with his uncle Bob.

When they got to us, I asked, "Can Cotton come to our house for a barbeque? Buddy's coming."

"If he wants to go, he can." Deputy Bob looked at the crowd. "I see I have work here, and Cotton can't go inside the jail now."

"A picnic at Maggie's beats all this craziness anyway," Cotton said.

"Be home before dark," Deputy Bob said to Cotton.

"I will."

I was happy to have my friends coming to my house for a picnic. I knew Mom wouldn't care if I had invited Cotton; she felt bad for him because his family left him. Well, his mother had. Nobody knew who his father was, so he had lived with his uncle ever since he was just a baby. Deputy Bob treated him real good.

"What y'all doin'?" Cotton asked.

I laughed. "You sound just like Buddy. We're going to a picnic, and we can play horseshoes or ball or whatever we like."

Buddy walked ahead with Charlie, so Cotton stayed by me. "They sure seem like they want to blame Wallis for what happened to Angel."

"Has your uncle said anything about it?" I asked.

"Not much, but he said the Walking Man isn't crazy like folks think. The doctors over at Tuscaloosa say he's eccentric, but there's no law against it."

"What y'all talkin' about?" Buddy hung back to walk with us.

"We're talking about Wallis." I said.

"What about 'im?"Buddy asked.

"There's nothin' wrong with him. My uncle says so, and Dinsdale says so too."

Charlie fell in step with us. "I never thought there was, but it looks like it's going to be hard to convince those people he's harmless."

"Well, they'll just have to accept it," Cotton said.

"My dad thinks he should be strung up," Buddy said. "He wants to string up all sorts of people. Niggers, as he calls 'em. Federal people, law officers. He's got a long list."

"I don't like the word 'nigger.' It makes me mad," I said.

"I'm not sayin' it, Maggie. It's what my dad says. You know how he can be."

"Just don't say it in front of me. Mozell's my friend, and that's a hurtful word to her, and I don't want to hear it again." I gave him a stern look.

"I didn't mean no harm, honest. Let's not fight." He put his arm on my shoulder.

Charlie lifted his BB gun and fired at a pine cone. It dropped to the ground.

"Good shot, Charlie." Cotton said. "Uncle Bob is going to get a new revolver from Deeter, and he promised to let me shoot it."

"You mean that Colt Deeter had?" I asked.

"That's the one."

"Well, that isn't going to happen. Me and Ida Mae were in his store yesterday, and somebody stole that gun."

"No! Are you sure?" Cotton asked.

"He looked all over the case, and it wasn't there. And he asked Randal if he sold it, and Randal said he didn't. Deeter was mad as hell."

"Maggie, watch your language, or I'll tell Mom." Charlie was acting real smart.

I squinted at Charlie. "He was mad, and he swore. I heard him."

"There are some strange things happening in town," Buddy said. "For sure Wallis didn't take it. He wasn't even here."

"Wait till Uncle Bob hears about this," Cotton said. "That's real odd. First we got a killer, and now we got a thief. What could be next?"

"If they find out who killed Angel," Buddy said, "there could be a hanging."

"That'll take a long time." Charlie fired again. "They don't even know who did it. They need some sort of clue. Do they have any?" He looked at Cotton.

Cotton pressed his lips together. "Not really. Uncle Bob said they were looking for something special Angel had on her but that they couldn't find it."

"Like what?" I asked.

"I don't know. Uncle Bob wouldn't tell me. You were there. What'd you see?"

"Yeah, Maggie. You and Charlie were there. What'd you see?" Buddy asked.

Cotton and Buddy were staring back and forth between me and Charlie. I thought for sure that Charlie would tell them about the cross, but he didn't say anything.

I said, "We just found her, and we didn't go close. I didn't even know she'd been murdered. I thought she fell off the log and hit her head. I don't have any idea what they might be looking for."

The rest of the walk to our house was kind of quiet. The boys took turns shooting Charlie's BB gun, and I hung back. I fingered the cross in my pocket and wondered if that was what they were trying to find. But maybe it was something else. I had kept it a secret for almost a week. Now I didn't know how I could tell anyone that I had found it. Sure, Charlie knew, but he had kept his promise not to tell. The secrets were getting harder to keep, and my stomach churned. I decided to go visit Mozell. I hadn't seen her for several days, and I wanted to see her and tell her all that was happening in Taneytown.

But that would be tomorrow. Today was a picnic.

❧   ❧   ❧

Our picnic was great fun. And I was right: Mom didn't mind that Cotton had come. Dad just put more chicken on the grill. We had tons to eat, and we talked and laughed and played horseshoes.

And for once, I beat Charlie and got to be the Grand Exalted. It was just wonderful.

CHAPTER 20

Monday was sunny and hot. I helped Mom do laundry in the morning, while it was still a little cool. My job was to hang the clothes on the line that ran alongside the house, towards the apple trees. I had to do it just so. All the underwear had to be together: Dad's and Charlie's in one section, mine and Mom's in another. Then the washcloths and towels were hung together, then the pants, and finally the shirts and Mom's dresses. Pajamas went wherever room was left, but they had to be neat. I didn't understand any of this, but it was the way Mom had been taught, and that's how she taught me.

Charlie came from the back porch, where he was helping Dad paint, and pointed to things. "You got a green sock with a black one. Better straighten that out. Neaten up my underwear, too."

I threw clothespins at him and yelled. He ran back around the house, but I knew he'd be back to tease me. My BB gun was close by, and I waited. Sure enough, he came back. He saw me aim the gun at him.

"You better not," he said.

"Don't come around here bothering me, or I'll shoot you in the butt."

"Gee whiz, Maggie. You sure are testy. Can't you take a joke?"

"Yeah. Can't you take a BB?"

As he turned away, he said, "You couldn't hit me anyway."

Why did he have to say that? I fired and hit him in the butt. He jumped back around with a stunned look on his face. "Dang you, Maggie. So you can shoot. Well, good."

I immediately felt bad. "I'm sorry, Charlie. You just make me so mad sometimes."

"Well, I hope you got that out of your system." He rubbed his butt. Then he grinned. "Been practicing?"

"Sort of. But that was a mistake."

"You called your shot. You hit it." He wiggled his lips. "I'm gonna go help Dad." He disappeared.

Tinker wandered over to me. "I can be dumb sometimes, Tinker, and mean too. That was mean, because I love Charlie. I'll have to find a way to make it up to him."

I leaned my Daisy against the maple tree in the front yard and went into the house. Tinker followed me. As I went into the kitchen, I asked, "Mom, can I go to Mozell's now?"

She was busy at the counter, mixing dough for a cherry pie. "Are the clothes all hung up?"

"Yes."

"You can go, but remember, no side trips. Just straight there and straight back." She sprinkled some flour on the dough and rolled it out again.

"I know. What are we having for supper?"

"Leftovers from yesterday. This pie will be done, and we'll have that too." She spread the flattened dough into a Pyrex dish.

"Mom?"

She stopped and looked at me. "What?"

"I love you and Dad and Charlie. And Tinker."

Her dark eyes searched mine. "Well, what brought this on?"

"I don't know. I just don't say it too often. Anyway, I do."

"I know. I love you too. Now, run along to Mozell's. The day's wasting." She smiled and went back to her pie.

I went into my room and got a nickel from my piggy bank. Charlie liked Baby Ruth candy bars, so I would get him one. I put the nickel into my jeans pocket, along with the cross. I went out to the maple tree and got my Daisy. The sun was blazing hot. I smelled paint fumes coming from behind the house, so I walked back to see what Dad and Charlie were doing.

They were on the porch, screening dozens of blank tiger boards that Dad had cut out in plywood. I had helped him coat the boards with white Sign Painter's 1 Shot. I knew the paint was expensive, but the silk screens cost a lot of money. Dad was real careful when he cut the patterns. The different screens would let one color at a time through the mesh. By the final pass, the orange and black tiger faces would appear. I watched Charlie work black paint through a screen with a rubber squeegee.

"You're getting black paint all over," I said. "That stuff's expensive."

Dad glanced up from the screen of orange that he was pressing and looked at me. "You want to help?"

"No, not now. I'm going to Mozell's."

"Some of these will be dry this afternoon. Then you can help put the different strands of wire on them." Dad picked up a finished tiger board that U.S. Steel had hired him to paint. It was the first finished one I had seen.

"It's pretty," I said. "But why is a smiling tiger holding steel wire?"

"It's just a display board." Charlie said. "See the easel on the back? That makes it stand up."

Dad laughed. He set the board down on the floor, and the tiger board stood upright, smiling at me and offering pieces of steel wire.

"I'll help put the wire on, but I'm not sure I get it." I stared at the tiger board.

"Have fun at Mozell's, and go straight there and straight back." Dad said.

"I know. Mom already said that."

He cleaned his hands on a gas-soaked rag and came over to me. He tugged on one of my pigtails. "You taking your BB gun?"

"Yes."

"Make sure you don't shoot things you're not supposed to."

He patted my head. I glanced at Charlie. He shrugged and rolled his eyes.

"Okay, Dad."

He gave me a little hug and then went back to the screening. Charlie was mouthing something, but I didn't know what, so I left. "Bye, Dad. Bye, Charlie."

"See you later, honey," Dad called.

It was like Dad could see everything. I didn't think Charlie had told him about the butt shot, but Dad knew. And I knew better than to do that again. Dad would let things go, unless you didn't catch his meaning the first time. Then you got a lecture. A long one. He talked, Mom used a switch. I preferred the switch.

As I walked down the hill, I shot at fence posts and sometimes even hit them. It was getting easier to sight the Daisy and hit what I aimed at, but I still needed a lot of practice. I decided I would go into the woods every chance I had and practice shooting pinecones off the trees. I wanted, just once, to beat Charlie at that game. Heck, he could even shoot mistletoe off the oak trees. I didn't know if I would ever be able to do that, but I sure would try my darnedest.

When I got to Main Street, I was happy that there weren't too many people walking around. Deputy Bob was sitting on a bench outside Sue Ann's, drinking an RC.

"Hi," I said.

"Hello, Maggie. How are you today?"

"Fine." I sat down beside him. "What's Cotton doing?"

"He's helping Mary with the twins. They can be a handful."

"I guess so." I studied his smooth, tanned face. "Has Wallis been arrested?"

"Not really. Why do you ask?"

"I don't think Wallis killed Angel, but a lot of folks do. Buddy says his dad wants to hang 'im."

Deputy Bob took a long drink of soda pop. "Well, Maggie, folks talk, but that doesn't mean much. Wallis is just Wallis."

"Is he still here?"

"We have him here for a while, till things calm down. Then he'll be free to go."

"Does he mind?" I asked. "About being locked up and stuff?"

"He isn't locked up, Maggie. He stays in one of the cells. He's got books to read, and Chief Dinsdale's wife sends over food."

"Gosh. He can read?"

Deputy Bob laughed. "Golly, Maggie. He's a reading fool. Reads everything we give him, but he likes science books the most. Books about stars and birds and things like that. I never saw anything like it."

I stared at Deputy Bob in wonderment. I never would have believed the Walking Man could read. And science books, at that. "Wait till I tell Buddy. Does Cotton know he reads?"

"Sure. He helped me pick some books for him this morning at the county library."

"Well, I'll be darned."

"You never know about people, now, do you?" He swallowed the last of his RC. "Where y'all goin'?" He put on his brown Stetson hat.

"Over to Mozell's place."

"I'll give you a ride to her road. I got to go over into Shelby county and see about something. You can get in the front seat, but don't touch anything." He took his bottle and went inside Sue Ann's grill.

I couldn't get to the car fast enough. Cotton got to ride in it sometimes, but I never thought I would. Charlie would be jealous as all get-out. I pulled the door open and slid onto the front seat. I rested my Daisy on the floorboard. The dashboard had all sorts of extra dials and switches attached to it. I knew they must be for the siren and the radio. I studied them real hard. It took all my strength to resist touching them.

Deputy Bob came out of Sue Ann's and got in. He smiled as he drove up towards Old Looney Mill, then turned around. He flipped a switch, and the siren blared. We drove through Taneytown, and people came out of Deeter's and the Valley Tavern and Sue Ann's and just about every store to look at us. I felt like a Santa riding on the fire truck. When we got to the bridge, Buddy was there fishing, and I waved. He about dropped his fishing pole. I grinned a big ol' grin, and he grinned back.

Deputy Bob flipped the switch off when we got to the highway. The siren wound down to a low whine and then stopped. He pulled off to the side of the road. "Be careful, Maggie."

I wanted to hug him, but I didn't. As I hopped out, I said, "Thanks. Cotton told me it was loud but fun. Thanks. Thank you, Deputy Bob."

"See you later, Maggie." He put the car in gear and drove off. I watched until he disappeared around a curve.

The sun beat almost straight down as I started along the dirt road that led to Mozell's. The corn had grown higher during the past week and now stood well over my head. It was so thick that patches of water from last week's rain had mosquito larvae floating on top. I for sure didn't want to be there when they all hatched.

I looked in the brush by the stream, expecting to see snakes, but I didn't see any. If I had, I would have shot at them. I didn't think they were something Dad would say not to shoot, but I wasn't sure. Sometimes, it was hard to be a kid.

Soon, I could see Mozell's house. She was not on the porch. I yelled, "Mozell!"

She stepped out and hollered to me. "Git on up here, honey girl! Mosquitoes will eat you alive." She went back inside.

She was right. They started biting me and buzzing in my face. Every time I slapped, blood flew. My arms looked like I'd picked a hundred sores. They nailed the hand carrying the Daisy and then got the other one. I ran as fast as I could up the steps and jumped inside the cabin. Mozell was seated at her table.

"Lordy, look at you." Mozell started laughing, and the tears rolled down her cheeks.

Her laugh was so happy that I started laughing. "They sure are mean," I said. "You have the meanest mosquitoes of anyplace."

"Oh, honey child, you knowed that's true." She wiped her face with a towel from her lap. "Now, sit by me and tell me what you been doin' besides slappin' yourself." She laughed again.

I leaned the BB gun against the wall and pulled a wooden chair next to her. "I haven't been doing much. I played with Ida Mae on Saturday, and we had a barbeque yesterday. My friends Buddy and Cotton came. We played horseshoes and sang, and stuff like that."

She took the towel and wiped the blood from my arms and face. "Sounds like you been doin' lotsa things." She stood. "I be forgettin' my manners. You want somethin' to eat? I ain't got no cookies. Willie and Maxine done ate 'em all."

"I don't need anything, Mozell."

"Sure you do. I got some fresh cornbread. It's sweet, too. Y'all want some buttermilk?"

"I'll have some cornbread, but I don't like buttermilk."

She rummaged in her small refrigerator and pulled out a stick of butter and the cornbread. "Don't have much sweet milk. I's got coffee left. Is you allowed to drink it?" She set the cornbread and the butter on the table.

"Sure. I have coffee with Mom almost every morning."

"Hmm, that so?" She got a heavy coffee cup from a wooden shelf and plunked it down. "I supposes you drink it black?"

"Mostly, but I'll have some milk in it today."

"That's probably a good idea." She poured sweet milk in my cup and just a little coffee.

"That's just right, Mozell."

"Thought so." She smiled and sat down. "Now, tells me about Miss Ida. How's that baby holdin' up?"

"She seems fine. She didn't cry or anything. She was giggling and laughing like she always did."

"Little ones seems to accept it best. She talk about Angel?"

I swallowed some cornbread and washed it down with the milk coffee. "Yeah. She talks out loud to her, like Angel is there."

"Hmm. Well, that may be true for her. Peoples we loves are always near us. Maybe we can't see 'em, but they be there." She swallowed a little coffee.

"I have something of Angel's." I said it before I even thought what I was saying.

"What's that?"

"Can you keep a secret?"

"I reckon I can. Ain't nobody out here to tell nothin' to, 'cept mosquitoes. Maybe some snakes." Her dark eyes twinkled.

I dug down into my jeans and laid the cross on the table. "This was Angel's."

Mozell picked up the gold cross and looked at it real close. "That's a pretty thing. How come y'all has it? Did she give it to you?" She laid it on the table.

"Not exactly."

"Not exactly, what?" She swirled her coffee cup.

"She didn't exactly give it to me." I chewed the last of the cornbread.

"You sure are presentin' a mystery. Like pullin' teeth. Out wid it, child."

"I found it. When I was showing Charlie the way to the waterfall, a crow was digging around in the pine needles. I chased him away, and there it was."

"Is you sure it's Angel's?" Mozell asked.

"I know it is, Mozell. I've seen it a million times around her neck."

"Suppose she lost it when y'all went up to the waterfall?"

"No, she had it on. I remember looking at her once when she was sitting on a log near the water, and the sunlight sparkled off it. I remember it plain."

"Hmm. Now what d'you suppose that means?"

"I don't know. Maybe whoever killed her took it and then lost it."

"Maybe. Shore is a mystery." She picked up the cross and looked at it again. "Dis is just like Joshua's tin box. You got somethin' will keep Angel wid you."

"I know."

"What else happenin' in town? I ain't heard nothin' lately."

I put the cross back into my pocket. "People keep coming to town and hanging around the jail and Sue Ann's grill."

"Lordy be. Now why would they do that? Don't sound like fun."

"The chief took the Walking Man over to Tuscaloosa right after Angel's funeral, and then he brought him back to the jail yesterday. Folks think he killed Angel."

"No!" Mozell fairly shouted. "Has they lost their mind? That man is the kindest person I know."

"You know him?" I couldn't believe it.

"I knowed him for a long time. Who you think chops my wood? This ol' body of mine ain't up to it. Folks is just plain crazy." She poured another cup of coffee for herself. "No wonder I ain't gettin' no news."

"He visits you?"

"Ain't you listen to me, child? Of course he do. Comes most every day. He gets mail for me. Tells me what's goin' on."

Now I understood why he went to the post office. "How come I haven't seen him here?"

"He's kinda shy. When he sees somebody he don't know, he vanishes. Just like a shadow on a cloudy day. Been that way his whole life."

"You know he reads?"

"Of course he do. Smart as a whip. Know most everything 'bout plants and stars. Tells me all 'bout 'em. Half the time, I falls asleep listenin', but he tells me things anyway."

"Gosh, Mozell. You got secrets too."

"That ain't no secret. I didn't see no reason to tell nobody about Wallis." She lifted my face to hers. "They put Wallis in the jail?"

"Yes, but they didn't arrest him. He sleeps in the cell, but the door isn't locked."

"Well, that don't make no sense." She sipped some coffee.

"Deputy Bob said they'll keep the Walking Man until all the fuss dies down. They don't think he killed Angel, and neither do I."

Mozell pressed her lips together and drank the last of her coffee. "It ain't right. He ain't done nothin'."

"The chief's wife sends him food, and they get him books."

"He must be scared, Maggie. He been wanderin' most of his life. Being in a jail ain't livin'."

"How come he wanders around?" I asked

"He be in a war, long time ago. I reckon it done things to 'im."

"Gosh. Seems like fighting in a war makes people strange," I said.

"Some it do, some it don't. Can't never tell." She patted my hand. "Well, you sure got news now, don't you? You better'n a newspaper."

"Seems like I'm learning an awful lot this summer. Some of it I don't even want to know."

"Can't grow if'n you don't learn." She carried her cup to the sink. "Y'all want more coffee?"

"No, I had enough. It was really good." I didn't want to tell her it was bitter even with tons of milk in it.

"You like my coffee, huh?"

"Yes."

"That's chicory. Grows up by the highway. Got dem blue flowers. You take some to your mama. Bet she ain't never had none." She put some dark roots into a small can and handed it to me. "She gonna have to grind."

"Thank you, Mozell."

"You my special child." She hugged me and stroked my hair. "It's gettin' towards noon, honey girl. Y'all needs to go, and you best run when you do it, cause dem bugs gonna want some of my cornbread, and dey can smell it on you. Bite, bite, bite." She laughed loud.

"Bye, Mozell. I'll be back real soon."

She bent to kiss my cheek. "Now, run along. Dis ol' lady got things to do."

I grabbed my Daisy and clutched the can of chicory roots tight against my chest. I jumped down the steps and ran like the devil was after me. I could hear Mozell laughing. The mosquitoes swarmed my face, but I couldn't do anything about it, because my hands were full. It was torture, but I reached the cornfield, and the mosquitoes just quit. They liked the shade, and I was glad. For once, I was thankful for the sun that beat down on me. "Scorch those damn things," I said aloud.

The sun was hot on the highway. Towards the bridge, I saw waves of heat rise from the pavement. I felt the heat through my Keds as I crossed the road. Orange and black butterflies flitted among the blue daisy-like flowers that lined the edge of the highway. I wondered if that was the chicory. Mozell knew all kinds of things about plants, because she ate a lot of them. I pulled a flower leaf from the prickly stems and bit it. It had to be chicory. It was bitter as all get-out.

I looked in the can and wondered if Mom would make coffee from the roots. Probably not. But you could never tell. I would take Mozell's gift to her anyway. As I neared the bridge, I saw Buddy was still fishing. "Hey, you catch anything?" I asked.

"No. Just little ones too dumb to know about stringy worms."

"Did you see me go by?"

"Yeah. What was that all about?" Buddy swung his cane pole towards the riverbank. The weighted line and wormy hook splashed into the water.

"Nothin'. Deputy Bob gave me a ride to Mozell's road. You see Cotton today?"

"No. I ain't seen nobody. Not even the Walking Man." He wiggled the line around in the water.

"Well, you won't see the Walking Man. He's in jail."

"No kiddin'?" Buddy turned to look at me. "Has he been arrested?"

"Deputy Bob says they're just keeping him for a few days. Did you know he can read?"

Buddy looked me straight in the face to see if I was fooling. "You tellin' the truth?"

"Yes. I wouldn't fool about a thing like that. Deputy Bob says he reads mostly science things."

"Well, ain't that somethin'? And here we all thought he was some kind of crazy person that didn't know nothin'." He shook his head. "Does Cotton know?"

"Sure does. He helped pick out some books for Wallis to read."

"Dang, Maggie. That takes all the mystery out. Who we gonna follow now?"

"Just because he reads doesn't mean he's not weird. He still dresses strange and acts kinda strange."

Buddy rubbed his red hair. "Are you still scared of 'im?"

"Maybe a little. But not a whole lot. Especially if he can read."

He lifted the cane pole over the edge of the metal bridgework and studied the empty hook. "Well, that was the last worm. Might as well go." He wrapped the line around the pole and said, "You sure like people that can read. Not everybody that reads can be trusted, Maggie."

"I know. But I never did think Wallis hurt Angel, and now that I know he can read, I truly believe he didn't hurt anybody ever."

Buddy smiled. "I sure am glad me and Cotton can read. It would hurt if you didn't like us."

"I would like you, Buddy Toliver, even if you didn't know your ABCs. So there."

Buddy looked at me but didn't say anything. We walked in silence to the river road that led to his house. He started down the roadway.

"So long, Buddy," I called.

"So long." He shifted the cane pole to rest on his shoulder.

I watched him go. Little puffs of red dust kicked up behind him as his bare feet plodded towards home.

CHAPTER 21

It wasn't much past noon when I walked through Taneytown. The door to the Valley Tavern stood open, and I could hear the familiar voice of Hank Williams coming from the jukebox. Men laughed, and glasses clinked above the strains of *Lovesick Blues*. The smell of hickory-smoked pork drifted along the sidewalk. I would have gone inside to get a sandwich, but I didn't have the money.

I had gone in once when I found a dollar, but I never told my mother. She would have been mortified to know, but heck, it wasn't scary or anything. The man at the counter was real pleasant. Nobody said anything to me. I sat on the stool at the long wooden bar and waited. When the sandwich came and I had paid my thirty-five cents, I loaded it with sauce and took my time eating. I never had one that good. I thanked the man, and he told me to come back. I knew I would, but not today. The nickel I had was for Charlie's candy bar.

I walked by the movie house and the barber shop and finally made it to Deeter's. The screen door squeaked as I pulled it open. Deeter was over by the gun case. "Hi, Deeter. What ya doin'?"

He smiled at me. "Just fixin' my cases so nobody else helps themselves to my guns."

I watched as he put hasps and locks on the cases. "You think that will do it?" I asked.

He finished screwing the last hasp on one of the wood frames. "It should." He slid the glass door shut and hooked a small padlock through the hasp ring. "Now, little missy, what can I do for you?"

"I need to buy a candy bar for Charlie."

Deeter walked towards the candy counter. "So you're buyin' some candy for your brother. Let me see. Did he beat you at doin' somethin', or are you just bein' nice to him?"

"Just being nice."

"I see." He spit tobacco juice into a tin cup. "Well, ain't that sweet of you? I see you got your Daisy with you. Been doin' any shooting?"

Damn, I thought, *does everybody know about my shooting Charlie in the butt?* They couldn't possibly know. "No. Just practicing some over in the woods by the river."

"Well, what will it be?"

"Charlie likes Baby Ruths."

"Then that's what he'll have." Deeter reached inside a case where he kept the candy bars and laid the Baby Ruth on the counter. "Five cents." He pushed the bar towards me. "Do you know if your dad has my sign ready?"

"I don't know, Deeter," I said as I put my nickel on the counter. "He and Charlie were working on some signs for U.S. Steel when I left this morning."

"U.S. Steel. Now, ain't that somethin'? Must be good money in that."

I didn't know if there was or not. Dad never talked about money. He just painted signs, and we helped him. "I'll tell him you asked," I said as I opened the screen door. "Bye."

When I went outside, Randal was parking his Crosley. I couldn't believe he had painted it again. Only a week ago, it was red, and now it was a purple kind of color. The paint looked wet, but I didn't stay long looking at it. I sure didn't want to take up a conversation with Randal. I heard the car door slam as I walked towards Oak Street.

Randal yelled, "Hey, little girl! Ain't you speakin' today?"

I turned back to him. "I got to get home."

"Don't shoot nobody with that little gun, hear?"

My face went red. Little gun? Boy, I'd like to shoot him with it and then have him call it a little gun. I knew that wouldn't happen, so I would just have to stay mad or get glad, as Mozell said. When I stomped across Oak Street, I looked towards Angel's house. Ida Mae was out on the sidewalk with her mother. They were clipping some roses. Ida Mae waved.

The sight of her grinning face made me smile. I yelled, "Hello, Ida! Hello, Mrs. Albright!"

Mrs. Albright waved, and they went back to gathering their red bouquet.

Ida Mae had taken the edge off my meanness, but I'll admit I did stop once or twice to shoot at some fence posts. And I did pretend they were Randal. I was glad when the BBs slammed into the wood, hard.

When I got to the top of the hill, Mom was taking the clothes off the line. "You want some help?" I asked.

She smiled at me as I crossed the yard. "No, Maggie, but your dad and Charlie could use some help. Most of the tiger boards are screened and dry. Dad is working on another project." She dropped more clothes into the basket.

"What's Charlie doing?"

"He's trying to put the steel strands on the boards, but you know he's not real handy with things like that."

"I know."

"Dad's been waiting for you to get home." She picked up the basket and started toward the house. "How's Mozell?"

"Fine. She sent you some coffee. We had some this morning." I looked at her to see if she was upset, but she didn't seem to be. "She calls it chicory. I had lots of milk with mine."

Mom laughed. "Oh, I see. Well, I'm sure you did."

"You ever have some?"

"Yes. And when I do, I have lots of milk with it."

Tinker followed us inside. "I never knew you to drink coffee any way but black," I said, as I set the can of chicory roots on the kitchen table.

Mom began folding clothes. "Anytime I have chicory coffee, I drink it with milk. Maybe you and I can have some tomorrow."

I smiled all the way to my room. Tinker followed me. Gosh, now I could drink coffee with Mom. I leaned the Daisy against my dresser. "See, Tinker?" I said. "I am growing up. I drink coffee, and I have my own BB gun." Tinker wagged her tail.

Mom yelled, "Maggie, go help your brother now! And be pleasant. He's worked hard all morning."

I went back to the kitchen. "Gosh, Mom. I bought Charlie a Baby Ruth, and I didn't even have to. I am nice to him."

She eyed me but didn't say anything. I wondered if she knew about the butt shot. I figured she did, but I didn't know how. Charlie's pride wouldn't let him tell. *Dang, parents know most everything,* I thought.

Charlie and I spent the rest of the afternoon putting five different-sized strands of steel wire on the tiger boards. The strands were about four inches long and had to be fastened with wire pulled through small drilled holes and twisted tight in the back. The twisting was the hard part. That's where Charlie had the most trouble. He was left-handed, and it seemed like he was all thumbs. I never could figure out how he could be so good at sports but could hardly swing a hammer without hitting his thumb.

"Slow down, Maggie." Charlie was chomping on his Baby Ruth.

"Well, gosh, can't you thread the wire faster? I'm just sitting here, waiting for you to do your part." I clanked the pliers open and shut, open and shut. I had taken over the wire twisting.

Charlie crammed the last of his candy bar in his mouth and licked his fingers. "How many more do we have to do, Dad?"

Dad was standing by his big plywood sign easel that hung from the posts supporting the back porch roof. He was putting the finishing touches on the sign for Deeter's store. "How many do you have done?"

"Hundreds."

Dad chuckled. "Well, that's a trick, since we only screened about seventy-five."

"It seems like hundreds." Charlie counted the racks. "We have over fifty done."

"Finish up a few more, and then you can quit. It's getting close to suppertime anyway."

Charlie winked at me. I knew he was happy to be almost done, because he had stuck the thin wire into his thumbs more than once. Drops of blood had smeared on some of the wire. "I'll do two more, and then I'm quitting."

"Maybe I'll stop too." I said. "Would you give me some more lessons in shooting my gun?"

"If you promise to aim at what I tell you, instead of other things."

I glared at him. He was just aching to tell Dad about the butt shot, but I thought Dad knew anyway, so I stuck out my tongue. "Just thread the wire, and try to do it right."

He smirked at me, and I couldn't help but laugh. In spite of myself, I loved my brother ... thumbs and all.

CHAPTER 22

Charlie and me didn't have much time to practice shooting, because Mom had supper ready right at 5:30, but he did show me more about sighting the rifle. I managed to shoot two pinecones off a tree behind our house. Charlie slapped me on the back. "There might be hope for you yet, Maggie," he said.

He wouldn't give me much, but I felt proud as we headed into the house. I would just keep practicing. One day, I would beat Charlie. When we went to the kitchen, Mom was putting the last of the leftovers on the table. "Where's Dad?" I asked.

"Finishing up on the porch. Go call him, Maggie." She set a pitcher of iced tea near my plate.

I walked out onto the back porch. Dad was cleaning his grey lettering quills in some gas and lathering them down with linseed oil. "Dinner's ready," I said.

"I'll be right there. Deeter's sign is almost dry, along with a few show cards I did for the Valley Tavern. After dinner, if you want, you and Charlie can go to town with me." He worked oil into the last of the fitches, then put the brushes, with the tips up, into a tin can. The oil ran into the heels. I loved how they smelled. Dad wiped his hands on a rag and asked, "Did you and Charlie make up?"

I was right. Somehow, he knew what I had done. "Yes." I continued, so he wouldn't say anything else, "Charlie and me were target shooting, and he showed me some better ways to aim."

"Charlie and I," he corrected me with a smile. "Come on. Let's eat."

He opened the back screen door, and we went into the kitchen. Charlie and Mom were waiting for us. Dad and I washed our hands, then sat down. We all joined hands, and Mom said a short prayer. Then she asked, "I know what Dad and Charlie did today, but what did you do, Maggie? Besides visit Mozell and drink chicory."

"Chicory?" Dad made a face. He didn't drink coffee, but he must have tasted it.

"Good stuff, huh, Dad?" I said.

"How come I never got to drink chicory?" Charlie asked. "How come Maggie gets to try all that stuff?"

"Well, if you want some, I can fix you some tomorrow morning. Maggie and I are having some for breakfast. With milk, of course." Mom took a drink of iced tea.

Charlie gave me a smirky look, and I pretended to be upset, but he was in for a surprise. I decided to rub it in some more. "I rode in a police car today, and the siren was blasting and everything."

"You did not," Charlie said. "Always making things up."

"No, I'm not. You can ask Deputy Bob when you see him. He gave me a ride to Mozell's, and Buddy saw us. So there."

Charlie looked at Dad. "Is she foolin'?"

"I don't know, Charlie. It sounds like she might be telling the truth." Dad took a bite of a pickled egg.

"I am telling the truth," I said.

"Well, you don't always." Charlie gave me a knowing look.

I kicked his leg under the table. "Excuse me," I said. "I was crossing my leg and didn't mean to touch you."

Charlie didn't say anything. He ate his chicken and stared at me. I knew the ride in the police car had got his goat. *Grand Exalted, my foot.*

"Who wants cherry pie?" Mom asked as she took some dishes to the sink.

"I do," I said, as I finished the last of my macaroni salad and chicken.

"Me too," Charlie said.

"I'll have mine later, Laura," Dad said. "Maggie, help your mom clean off the table, and as soon as you and Charlie are done, we'll load up the station wagon and take the signs to town." He gave Mom a kiss, then went to the back porch.

Charlie and I ate our pie in silence. Mom didn't have any pie. I figured she and Dad would have theirs later. Sometimes I thought they just wanted to be alone together, without me and Charlie bothering them, but they never said that. I just thought it sometimes.

When Tinker whined, I gave her a piece of my pie crust. Then I gathered up the remaining dishes and took them to the sink. Mom stopped washing and hugged me for no reason. It made me feel good.

"Come on, Charlie. Let's go," I said.

He finished the last bite of his pie and pushed away from the table. "Thanks, Mom. That was good." Then he looked at me. "Let's go, policewoman."

Dang. He could make me mad so quick, but I sure wouldn't show it. "Don't get smart," I said. Secretly, I was glad he was jealous.

Dad had already put the poster boards for the Valley Tavern in the back seat. Charlie helped him carry the big wooden sign for Deeter's, and I kept Tinker out of the way while they loaded it and some tools into the back.

"Can I sit in front?" I asked.

"It's my turn," Charlie said.

Dad looked at us and scratched his head. "I don't remember whose turn it is. There's room for both of you up front." Charlie and I stared at one another.

"You first, Maggie," Charlie said.

"I want the window."

I stood my ground. Charlie didn't budge.

Dad started the engine. "If you're going, get in. I can't hang around until this is settled."

I slid in next to Dad, and Charlie sat by the window. I didn't care—not really. But just the same, I said to Charlie, "Don't touch me."

He and Dad laughed.

"What's so funny?"

"Not a thing, Maggie. Sometimes you just tickle me." Dad put the car in gear, and we started towards Taneytown.

Charlie hugged the open window and let his arm and hand soar in the wind. He didn't try to touch me, and I was glad. I didn't want to fight.

When we got to town, I was surprised to see dozens of men and even some women standing around the jailhouse. There had been hardly anyone along the street when I had walked through earlier. Dad slowed the car to look at the group. He had to park down near the movie house, because the streets were full of cars and trucks.

"You kids wait here a minute. I'll take the posters into the tavern and be right back."

Charlie and me stood on the sidewalk, looking towards the jail. "Those people look mad." Charlie said.

"I hope it's not about the Walking Man. He didn't do anything. Cotton told me so. Besides, he can read."

"He can read?"

"Well, yeah. What's so odd about that? He's smart, and he reads science stuff."

Charlie looked like he didn't believe me.

"Well, it's true. Everybody knows it. Except you, I guess." I gave him a sweet smile.

As we stood there looking, more people drove up in their trucks. Since there were no parking places, they just parked in the street. The voices were getting louder and louder.

Dad came out of the tavern and looked towards the jail. "Let's take that sign to Deeter's. We might have to hang it tomorrow."

Charlie and Dad pulled the plywood sign out of the station wagon, and I shut the tailgate. I followed them but kept my eyes on the jailhouse. Deeter had come out and was looking at the growing crowd. He stood with his hands on his hips and then spit tobacco juice into the gutter. "Looks like we might have a lynchin' if things don't calm down."

"We'll hang the sign tomorrow, Deeter, if that's okay," Dad said.

"Sure. This could get ugly." He kept his eyes on the crowd.

Just then, a dusty pickup slammed to a stop in front of the jail. Buddy's dad jumped out with two other men. They were the same men I had seen the day me and Cotton, Buddy, Angel, Ida Mae had been near their whiskey still.

Buddy's dad climbed up on the back of the truck. He held a rope in his hands. "Y'all know why you're here. That slimy, dirty old man ain't goin' to get away with killin' that pretty little thing."

People in the crowd shouted and raised their fists. The men who came with Alton pulled shotguns out of the truck cab. I got scared.

"Chief Dinsdale!" Alton yelled. "Git on out here, and let us do our job. You ain't got no right to help that son of a bitch. You know he done it."

Others in the crowd chanted, "Hang 'im, hang 'im." More and more people began yelling and hollering. My dad looked pained.

In the crowd, the man called Mark stood near Sue Ann's grill. He looked calm as he smoked a cigarette. The blond woman with the big chest leaned against him, clinging to his arm.

About then, I saw Willie's car stop behind Alton's truck. Mozell and Willie got out. Mozell had on a pure-white dress and the prettiest white beaded hat I ever saw. It was tall and round and looked like a crown. I was absolutely amazed. I had never seen Mozell in town before. She walked right up to the truck. Willie stayed back by the car.

I don't know what it was, but for a moment, the crowd stopped their shouting and simply stared at her. Mozell was like a black angel. "Mista Alton," she said, "you messin' wid the wrong person. That man inside is good. He ain't done nothin' to hurt nobody."

Buddy's dad got the ugliest look on his face. He spit out, "What the hell does a nigger have to say about all this? You get the hell back to the bottoms where you come from, nigger, or you'll be next—along with that skinny nigger back by the car." He shook the rope at Willie.

"Dad, don't let them hurt Mozell. Dad, please." I was near tears.

Dad looked at me, but he didn't move.

I don't know what got into me, but I jumped off the curb and ran to Mozell. "Leave her alone. Leave her alone!" I yelled.

The door to the jailhouse opened. Buddy ran out, followed by Cotton and Deputy Bob. Deputy Bob had a shotgun, but he didn't get a chance to use it.

One of the men with Buddy's dad hit Deputy Bob on the head with the barrel of his shotgun, and Deputy Bob went down. He was knocked out by the blow.

Buddy began yelling, "Damn you! You always got to bully everybody. Well, you got it wrong. Me and Cotton know the Walking Man wasn't even there on the day Angel got killed, but you were. You and those two shotgun thugs." He pointed to the men.

Mozell shouted, "Mista Wallis Walker was wid me that day, choppin' wood! You done got it wrong."

Alton looked at Buddy. "What the hell are you sayin', boy?"

"I saw you and that blond woman foolin' round by that whiskey still." He pointed to the blond woman hanging on Alton's boss's arm. She gasped. Mark jerked her around, and they started arguing.

The crowd bobbed their heads towards the couple and then bobbed back to Mr. Toliver. He shouted, "You never saw no such thing! You're lyin'!"

"I know what I saw. You chased us with shotguns, and then Angel come up missin'."

Alton's face turned a purplish red, and the veins bulged in his skinny neck. He jumped down from the truck and started hitting

Buddy with his fist. Buddy tried to defend himself, but he was no match. The crowd was shouting.

I couldn't stand it. I kicked Mr. Toliver's legs and hit him as hard as I could, but it didn't seem to hurt him at all. He had hold of Buddy with one hand and was slapping him with the other. Mozell tried to pull me away, but I fought her and kept kicking. "Stop it. Stop it!" I cried. "You're killing him!"

The crowd began yelling for Mr. Toliver to leave Buddy alone, but he kept on hitting him.

I don't know where my dad came from, but suddenly he was there. He caught Mr. Toliver's fist in his hand and spun him around. Mozell jerked me back, and I stared at my dad in amazement. I never knew him to be in a fight.

"You coward, you," my dad said. "You lousy coward." He let fly a right upper hook that would have made Joe Louis proud.

Mr. Toliver went stiff. Then he dropped like an ol' sack of potatoes.

"Lordy be," Mozell said.

The two men that had come with Mr. Toliver moved towards my dad. He started to raise his fists, but he was hit in the face with a shotgun barrel. The blow sent him staggering back, a trickle of blood flowing from his cheek. The crowd grew quiet.

From behind us came the sound of screeching tires. A door opened, and a loud shotgun blast filled the air. "Stop all this right now." Chief Dinsdale elbowed his way through the crowd and fired another blast. *Boom!*

Everyone moved aside. There was total silence.

Deputy Bob sat upright at the sound of the second shotgun blast. He staggered to his feet. "I wasn't going to let them get in the jail. It was getting real ugly. But I got hit by that man." He pointed to the heavyset man.

Dinsdale eyed the pair.

"The boys have told me quite a story." Deputy Bob pointed at Mr. Toliver. "You need to talk to him and these two men."

Chief Dinsdale pointed his shotgun at the men. "Put those guns back in the truck, boys, and step inside my place. And drag your friend with you."

The two men looked at him for only a moment, then they put their weapons on the front seat of Mr. Toliver's truck. The heavier man grabbed Alton's collar and dragged him towards the jail. Deputy Bob followed them inside.

The chief turned to the crowd. "The party's over. There ain't nothin' to do but go home. The law will handle this in due time."

There was a little mumbling. Someone said, "Well, I never. You think Alton done it?" They walked real slow back to their cars and pickups.

Willie said, "Come on, Mama. Let's git out o' here. I be scared. These folks is crazy."

Mozell pulled me to her. "You don't have to worry 'bout your secret no mo'. It's out of your hands now." She patted my head. "Lordy, girl. You shore can fight. Your daddy not bad either." The black angel turned and walked back to Willie.

Dad called, "Come on, Maggie. We need to get home."

"In a minute, please. I need to talk to Buddy."

"Hurry, then." Dad walked toward Deeter's store.

I didn't see Buddy anywhere. Cotton stood on the sidewalk like he was in shock. "Cotton?" I asked. "Where's Buddy?"

"I don't know. He must have slipped away." He looked around.

"He was terrible beat. I hope the chief locks his dad up forever."

Cotton said, "I'm sorry, Maggie, about not keeping your secret. But see, Buddy heard his dad talking to those men about hanging the Walking Man, and he came to see me. That's when I told him what you saw the day Angel was killed."

"It's all right."

"We decided to tell Uncle Bob about the plan to hang Wallis, and we did."

"Is Wallis still in jail?" I asked.

"Heck, no. Chief Dinsdale slipped him in his car earlier and took him down the highway towards his home. Nobody knows for sure where he lives, except up in the mountains. That's where the chief was."

"Does he know about the whiskey still?"

"Dinsdale was gone by the time Buddy and me got here, so he doesn't know about anything we told Uncle Bob. Pretty soon he will, though."

"Was Deputy Bob mad?"

"Not mad, Maggie. Maybe a little disappointed because we didn't tell the truth to start with. But he isn't mad at us." Cotton kicked stones off the sidewalk.

"Where do you suppose Buddy went?" I asked.

"I don't know. He won't go home, though. Not if he thinks his dad will be there."

A shrill whistle came from across the street. My dad was calling. "I got to go, Cotton. Maybe I'll see you tomorrow. I sure hope I see Buddy."

"See ya, girl." Then Cotton did something he had never done before. He hugged me. "You are a true friend." He turned quick like and went into the jailhouse.

After the door shut, I went across the street to Charlie and Dad, and we walked down to the station wagon. The marquee lit up as we passed the movie house, and I could smell popcorn.

When we drove back through town, it was mostly deserted, except for a few people sitting outside Sue Ann's. Deeter and Randal stood in front of the store and waved as we rode past. By the time we got home, Dad's cheek was swollen, and he had a ragged cut on his right hand. Mom was just beside herself when she saw him.

"Oh, John, what in the world happened? Did you fall off the ladder?" She clung to him as he went to the kitchen sink.

Dad splashed water on his face and scrubbed his hands over and over with soap and hot water. "Well, Laura, falling off a ladder might have felt better, but that's not what happened." He winked at Charlie and me. "I think I'll have my cherry pie now."

"Come on, Charlie. Let's go outside," I said.

For once, Charlie didn't argue with me. We went outside and sat on the porch steps. Tinker sat between us, pushing against us, begging to be petted. We watched the sun set behind a mountain towards Birmingham. The clouds turned orange and pink and yellow. Then the sun was gone, and darkness came over us. Fireflies twinkled here and there along the hillside.

"Gosh," Charlie said, "I knew you could fight, but I never thought Dad could. I never saw him that mad."

"Me neither. You suppose that's why he doesn't whip us when we're bad?"

"I never thought about it." He patted Tinker's head.

"I never did either. I guess I'd rather have his long lectures than feel his hand on my butt."

Charlie smiled. "Dad sure had us fooled. Just think! He could have blistered us easy a lot of times. We sure are lucky to just have Mom's feathery switchin'."

The fireflies flashed by the hundreds now. "Go get a jar, Charlie. Let's catch lightning bugs."

Charlie laughed as he went into the house. In a few minutes, he came out with a Ball canning jar. He and I and Tinker ran down the hill towards the barbeque pit, chasing the lights of summer.

"You want to see who can catch the most and be Grand Exalted?" Charlie asked.

"Not tonight. Let's just catch what we can and then let them go. I don't want to work at it."

"Okay."

We ran and jumped and caught the glowing bugs with our hands and put them in the jar. It felt wonderful to be a kid again.

CHAPTER 23

The next morning was bright with sunshine. I woke up happy, because so much had changed. I no longer had to worry about my lies, thanks to Buddy and Cotton. I still hadn't told anyone except Charlie and Mozell about the cross, but it didn't seem to matter. Chief Dinsdale had put Mr. Toliver and the two men in jail for what happened to Angel, and the Walking Man was free to wander again.

I thought about Buddy as I was getting dressed, and wondered how he was and if he had gone home. Now he didn't have to be scared anymore. His mean old father couldn't get to him. It just made me smile.

When I went out to the kitchen, Dad was sitting at the table, drinking milk and having a piece of cherry pie. "Morning, Maggie." His face was swollen, and he had a black eye.

"Gosh, Dad. I hardly know you. Does it hurt?"

"Not really. My hand does, and it looks like I won't be painting signs for a few days." His hand was bandaged and looked puffy too.

Mom came from their bedroom. She was still in her night-clothes. I was sort of surprised, because she seldom had breakfast in her nightgown, not even on Christmas morning. "You sick?" I asked.

"No, I just slept late." She smiled as she took a carton of eggs out of the refrigerator. "Who wants bacon and eggs?"

"I do," Charlie said, as he came into the kitchen.

"Me too," I said.

"I'll have some," Dad chimed in.

While Mom got the bacon and eggs ready, I gathered dishes and silverware. Life seemed back to normal, and the fears of the past week were all behind. I thought about Ida Mae then. For her family, things would never be the same. I wondered how it felt to lose a sister or a brother. I looked at Charlie. Sometimes he could make me so mad that I wanted him to disappear, but I had never thought about the forever part. That's the part I couldn't get a hold on.

"What are you going to do about the tiger boards, Dad?" Charlie asked.

"Not much for several days. Maybe we could go fishing. I know it's not good right now, but it might be nice to just float."

"Can I go?" I asked.

Charlie answered before Dad could say anything. "I reckon I'd be proud for you to go, seein's how you whopped on Mr. Toliver."

"Well, somebody had to." I felt proud that Charlie had complimented me. "Anyway, Dad finished it."

Dad smiled. "I'm not sure it was worth not being able to paint, but at least Buddy got away."

"Nobody knows where he went. I asked Cotton, and he didn't know," I said.

"Ah, he'll show up. Buddy's tough," Charlie said.

Bacon sizzled in the black iron skillet. Mom poured the eggs into another frying pan and began stirring. "I hope scrambled eggs are okay. I don't feel up to specialties this morning."

"What about our chicory coffee?" I asked.

"Oh, yes. I almost forgot. Three cups, right?"

"Yes, and make Charlie's the biggest."

"Gee, Maggie, how come you're being so nice to me?" Charlie asked.

"Because I'm just a nice person." I smiled sweetly.

Both Mom and Dad laughed out loud.

❦   ❦   ❦

The next few days moved slow like. Dad, Charlie, and me went fishing up at Lake Purdy, and we even caught some bass. Charlie, of course, caught the biggest one, and I got to hear all about the power of the Grand Exalted over the little peons. I tried not to listen too hard.

I loved being in the wooden boat we rented, just drifting along the edge of the lake, trying to catch fish with my casting rod. Dad preferred a fly rod, and he could lay a line out twenty yards or more, just as smooth as could be. His time growing up in Pennsylvania along mountain streams had made him a lifer with a fly rod. Sometimes I would try my hand at it, but I seemed bent on throwing the feathery fly into brush. Dad would have a devil of a time getting it unstuck. Charlie, of course, would laugh. But I didn't care if he laughed, because that's just the way Charlie was. I suspected that's how all brothers acted. Anyway, it didn't seem mean.

The day we went fishing, Mom visited with Mrs. Albright. She told us later that they had taken Ida Mae into Birmingham to go shopping and to have lunch at the Britling. I was glad I had gone with Charlie and Dad. I loved the macaroni and cheese at the Britling, but somehow our baloney and mustard sandwiches tasted really good. It was a perfect day.

The next morning, Charlie and me went into town to Deeter's store. I carried my Daisy, because I was determined to practice until I could beat Charlie at shooting pinecones off the pine trees. I needed to get more BBs, and Charlie wanted to buy a fishing magazine. Deeter had a scowl on his face as we came in the door.

"What's wrong, Deeter?" I asked.

"That dang Randal. He doesn't show up when he's supposed to. I had to put up stock, and I'm gettin' too old for that." He rubbed his arms.

I saw Dad's sign leaning against the shelves near the front window. I said, matter-of-factly, "Dad hurt his hand. He won't be able to put the sign up for a few days."

"I figured that," Deeter said. "It'll wait."

Charlie went over by the magazine rack and pawed through the titles. "Why don't you fire Randal?" he asked.

"Damn, I should. But there ain't nobody else wants to work for me. I'm too ornery, I guess." He spit tobacco into a can on the counter.

"Maybe he's painting his car again," I offered.

"That's another thing. Ain't that strange?" Deeter asked.

"I think a lot of things are strange," Charlie said, as he leafed through a *Field and Stream,* "but then they don't turn out that way."

"Like what? You mean the Walking Man?" I asked.

"Maybe." He studied something in the magazine closely. "Maybe how things happen."

"What are you talkin' about, boy?" Deeter asked.

"Well, you know. Like … you think things are all settled, and then they aren't. It's like a trick."

Deeter studied him. "I don't get it."

"He sometimes talks in circles," I said. "Don't pay any attention to him." It was like Charlie didn't even hear us talking about him.

I shrugged. "I need two tubes of BBs."

"Well, I know one thing," Deeter said as he pulled two tubes off the shelf. "Alton Toliver is sure in a mess of trouble. Who would have believed that?" He plopped the BBs on the counter. "Anything else, Maggie?"

"I think I'll get some candy." I walked along the cases, studying the selection.

"That's part of what I mean," Charlie said. "Whiskey and women." He put the *Field and Stream* on the counter. "How much?"

"Lord have mercy, boy. You don't make no sense." Deeter rubbed his nose. "That'll be twenty-five cents."

"You got any money, Maggie?" Charlie asked. "I only got two dimes."

"Golly, Charlie. Five cents would get five pieces of candy."

"Well, I'll pay you back. Can you help me or not?"

I eyed him hard, then handed him a nickel. "You're welcome, mister."

He grinned. "Thanks." He gave the nickel to Deeter. "Feisty, huh?"

"I reckon so," Deeter said. "You gonna have any candy, Maggie?"

I only had twelve cents. "Yeah, a pinwheel and a piece of licorice."

"Black or red?" Deeter asked.

I looked at Charlie. "Well, mister, which one?"

"Black," Charlie said.

Deeter kind of rolled his eyes as he handed the licorice to Charlie and the pinwheel to me. "You two have an understandin', I reckon, but it beats me."

I laid my money on the counter and took the two packs of BBs. "Bye, Deeter." Charlie and me walked out to the street. I turned to go down towards the river.

"Hey, Maggie. I thought you were going home." Charlie said.

"No, I want to do something." I didn't want to tell him I was going to practice shooting, because he might want to go along. I didn't want him to.

"Be careful, Sis." He sucked on his licorice stick.

"I always am. Besides, there's no reason to be scared anymore." I pointed towards the jail. "They're locked up for what they did to Angel."

"Maybe."

"Well, they are."

Charlie bit into his candy. "There's a difference between whiskey and women and children."

"That's the dumbest thing I ever heard you say. Of course I know that."

"You just be careful. If something happens to you, I won't have anybody to fight with." He laughed and then turned toward home.

I stood looking after him. I thought, *Now, why does he talk in riddles, and on today, of all days?* Here I was feeling relieved, and he had to go and stick a dumb ol riddle in my face. Most times, I understood Charlie, but sometimes I figured he just said odd things to rile me up. I decided I wouldn't let him get my goat.

There weren't many people on the streets. A few milled around the post office, and some were sitting on the benches outside Sue Ann's. Mostly, the streets seemed normal—empty, with only a few cars here and there. As I walked towards the movie house, a dark-blue Ford coupe pulled up to the curb. Mrs. Turner, Randal's mother, was inside. I called, "Hi."

She stepped out, smiling. "Morning, Maggie. It's a wonderful day, isn't it?"

"Sure is," I said.

"You going hunting?"

"No. Just target shooting."

"Well, you be careful with that little rifle, dear. They've been known to hurt folks."

It was all I could do to muster a "Yes, ma'am." But I did. I walked away, and she headed towards Deeter's Store.

The smell of barbeque coming from the tavern made me feel good. I wished I had remembered to bring more money, but I hadn't, so a barbeque sandwich would have to wait. I looked inside the doorway as I walked by, and someone waved, but it was so dark in there I couldn't see who it was.

As I approached the bridge, I looked for Buddy, but there was no one around. I stepped off the pavement to the right and headed down the dirt road that followed the river. When I got to the willow, I jumped the ditch and walked about twenty yards into the pines.

The trees towered above me like green giants. I loved the smell. I studied the trees to see which one had the most cones, and chose one that seemed taller than all the rest. If I could shoot those cones down, I would be able to hit almost anything. One day, Charlie would be in for a real surprise.

I unscrewed the shot tube and loaded the Daisy with BBs. I cocked the lever and took careful aim. *Bam.* Missed. I cocked it again, and again. I must have fired over twenty times, but I only knocked four pinecones out of the tree. It was harder than I had imagined, but I was determined to get it right. I wished Buddy or Cotton was there to give me pointers. It was all up to me, so I kept firing. I shot for a long time.

I didn't hear the footsteps that came from the hill behind me until they were real close. I expected maybe Cotton had found me. I swung around and was stunned to see Randal. His right hand was behind his back. He smiled at me. I inched away, towards the road.

He had splatters of red paint on his yellow shirt and his faded jeans. I thought it odd that his shirt was buttoned to the neck. "What ya doin'?" he asked.

"Just practicing. But I'm done."

"You want to shoot a real gun?"

For a moment, a wave of friendliness came over me, but it passed. "I don't think my dad would like that," I said.

"He won't know. C'mon."

"I don't think so. Really, Randal. But you can shoot. I'll just watch for a few minutes, and then I have to go."

He studied my face. "You ain't scared, are you?"

"No," I lied, with my best smile.

He brought out his right hand, and I was amazed to see the Colt that had been stolen from Deeter's. I swallowed hard and tried to keep my face from showing what I knew. "Ain't this a beauty?" he asked.

"It sure is."

"Watch this, now. I learned how to shoot during the war. I killed lots of krauts." He aimed at a pinecone high up and fired. The sound was so loud that I almost screamed. The cone dropped to the ground. Randal unbuttoned his shirt collar with his left hand. "This damn thing is too tight," he said. "Interferes with my aimin'."

He turned towards me, and I saw something hanging around his neck—something I never thought I'd ever see again. "You got Angel's necklace," I blurted out. "You got her necklace!"

He looked stunned for a moment as he fingered the chain. "You don't know what you're talking about."

"Yes, I do. I know that necklace. You must have killed Angel. You did it, and I'm tellin' Chief Dinsdale."

Randal got a mean look on his face. "You ain't goin' nowhere."

He started towards me. I just raised my Daisy and fired. The BB didn't hit him where I hoped it would. It caught him in the throat, just above the necklace. His mouth opened in a wide gasp, but no sound came out. He staggered backward and dropped the Colt.

I ran like the devil was after me. I heard him scrambling in the pine needles for the gun. If he got it, I knew I couldn't outrun the shot he would fire; he was too good. I jumped out on the road, into the sunlight. I prayed that someone would be there, but the road was empty and no longer safe.

I yelled for help and kept running. I ran a few yards down the dirt road and then dodged towards the riverbank and went down a path through the brush. I threw my Daisy on the rocks along the water's edge.

I heard him jump the ditch. He fired. The shot crashed through the brush but didn't hit me. I took a deep breath and dove in the water, clothes and all. I would swim as fast and as far as I could. I thought about all the times me and Charlie had played this game. If I lost this time, it would be my last.

Even underwater, I could hear shots hit the water. I swam and swam until I thought my lungs would bust, but I kept going. I pulled myself along the bottom by grabbing onto rocks. The river seemed so wide and the other bank so far away. I prayed that God would get me to the other side. My eyes were wide open, and I saw mullets swim by. They scared me, but Randal and the gun scared me more. When I thought I couldn't last another second, I saw the roots of brush that grew along the bank. I grabbed at them. Then a hand grabbed mine.

I was jerked up, gasping for breath. The first person I saw was Buddy. His face was all red and splotchy, and one eye was black and blue with yellow rings. Then I looked into the face of the Walking Man. He had pulled me out, and we were deep in the brush. "You got friends now, little girl," he said.

"Oh, Buddy. I'm so scared. He killed Angel. Randal killed Angel!"

Buddy put his arms around me. "How do you know? Is that why he was shooting at you?"

"I saw the necklace. I got Angel's cross, and he has the necklace. He did it. I told him I knew he did it, and that's why he was trying to kill me."

The Walking Man whispered, "We best get away from here. We'll slip over to Mozell's. She'll know what to do."

Buddy peered through the brush towards the other side of the river, then stood up. "I think he's gone." He crouched back down. "I still don't understand."

"I found the cross when me and Charlie were going to the water-fall. But the necklace was missing."

Buddy sighed. "I'll bet that's what Deputy Bob meant about something special of Angel's."

As the Walking Man stood, he put his black hat back over his wild mess of brown-and-grey hair. "Best go," he said. He motioned us toward the highway. Me and Buddy followed him, just like we had a million times before. It was hard to keep up, but we did. The corn was even higher along the road that led to Mozell's. I was still scared, but I felt safer when I saw her come out on her porch.

"Well, looky at dis comin'. A scarecrow, a beat-up boy, and a drowned-lookin' girl. What in the world has ya'll been doin'?"

Mozell made me smile. Buddy laughed. The Walking Man tipped his hat. "We'll be visiting a while. Till things cool down. Then we'll go to town."

"I's got some cookies and some tea. Then ya'll can tell me all about your doins today. You two ain't been gone long, so somethin' happened. It best be good, cuz I ain't feedin' ya unless you got somethin' good to tell."

"What's she mean about you not bein' gone long?" I asked.

"Never mind, now. I'll tell you later, maybe," Buddy said.

The Walking Man sat down on the steps, and Buddy hopped onto the swing. I studied Buddy's face, but he gave me a blank look, so it was no use to push him any further for an explanation. I followed Mozell inside and watched her fix the tea. She didn't have much ice, but I didn't care. I was just happy to be there. She put the full glasses on a tray and motioned towards the green bread box. It was heavy with cookies.

After we gave Buddy and Wallis their tea, Mozell took her favorite side of the porch swing. I slid in between her and Buddy. "Now, ya'll nappy-lookin' folks needs to tell me why ya'll looks so messed up," she said.

Buddy and me took our time telling what had happened. Mozell didn't say much except, "I see," "Uh, huh?" and "Lordy be."

If Charlie and Cotton had been there, it would have been a perfect afternoon, but they would have their fun later, listening to all that had happened. I didn't even care that I had lied to Dinsdale. I figured he would understand. Maybe.

I fingered the cross in my pocket and stole sideways glances at the Walking Man. Wallis just sat listening to Buddy and me retell the story of when all of us had gone to the waterfall and then on to the whiskey still. Mozell was amazed about the part where the men had fired shotguns at us.

"Lord have mercy, child. Ya'll was lucky to make it out alive. Seems like dem guns is bad for folks. 'Cept maybe yours, Maggie. It done saved you." Mozell squeezed my arm and pushed the swing into motion.

Then I told about how Charlie and me had found Angel. I felt like I could see it all again. It had never really seemed like it had happened until that moment. Sometimes I felt like I could change that day, and then Angel would be all right. But when I said out loud how she had looked lying in the mud and how the woods had seemed dark and empty, I finally knew I'd never see her again. Something happened inside me, and I busted out crying.

Buddy hugged me. "It's okay, Maggie. It's okay."

Mozell stroked my head. "Ya'll needs to shed yourself of them tears. They like crossin' a river. First come the fast part, and den the river flows peaceful-like. You done started down the rapids. Now you needs to reach the slow, smooth part. Y'all feel better once you git to the other side."

I don't know how long I cried, but after a while, I felt better. "I want to go now and tell what Randal did."

Buddy moved off the swing. "I'll go with you, Maggie. I seen what he done. The shootin' at you when you swam under the water."

"I'll walk you to the bridge, Missy." Wallis stood and tipped his hat to me.

His high, thin voice startled me. Then I looked into the Walking Man's blue eyes. They seemed like the kindest eyes I had ever seen. I knew then that our game of following "the witch" was over. Somehow I didn't mind. "I'd be proud to have you do that, Mister Wallis Walker."

He smiled at me.

Buddy and me and Wallis went down the porch steps and out onto the dirt road. Mozell called, "Be careful. I don't want nothin' bad happenin' to my family."

I waved to her, and then we headed towards Taneytown. When we got to the cornfield, the sunlight felt good. At first, I thought it was because I was still wet. The more I thought about it, though, I knew something had changed for me. It seemed like the warmth came from somewhere beside the sun. It just felt different. I felt different.

CHAPTER 24

A police siren wailed as we stepped onto the highway. I looked towards the sound and saw Chief Dinsdale's car slow down as it rattled across the bridge. It skidded as it turned on the highway and headed north towards Birmingham. The siren screeched.

"What d'you suppose that's all about?" Buddy asked.

"How should I know?" I said. "Today is full of all sorts of surprises."

"Dang. Maybe we should have just run right to town, instead of going to Mozell's. Then we'd know what's happening."

The Walking Man didn't say anything.

"Well, I'm still scared about Randal," I said. "Suppose he's waiting for us? Then what are we going to do? The chief left. Maybe we should wait." I stopped walking just as we got to the bridge.

Buddy looked defiant. "We can't hide forever. Besides, there's three of us, ain't there? Randal ain't goin' to kill us all."

I got indignant. "Buddy Toliver, have you no sense? He's got that great big ol' gun, and he already showed me that he can shoot better than you and Charlie put together."

"Well, you got away. We could too. Maybe."

While Buddy and me fussed, the Walking Man had walked onto the bridge. He stood there, looking towards town. I stopped talking and watched him. Buddy stopped his fussing. "What's he doing?" he asked.

"I don't know."

Wallis turned and motioned for us to come. He had a smile on his face. "It'll be okay. There's lots of people on the streets. Go now."

We walked to where he stood. We could see that dozens of folks were all along the streets. It made me feel better. I knew we would be all right. Randal wouldn't dare try to hurt us now.

"C'mon, Buddy. We'll go straight to the jailhouse and tell what we know. Deputy Bob might still be there."

Buddy held back. "My dad is in there. I don't want to see him."

"He's locked up. He can't hurt you anymore."

Buddy ran his hand over his freckled, swollen face. "He done made me black and blue. You can go inside, but I ain't."

Wallis touched Buddy's shoulder. "He did you wrong, boy, but you got to go. You have a chance to be better." He patted Buddy's shoulder, and then he turned and walked back towards the highway. I suppose he headed for wherever he lived. The tails of his black coat billowed with a gust of wind. I don't know why, but I thought of Ida Mae and her little song. But in my head, the words came different:

> *The witch, the witch, the walking witch,*
> *He grabbed my hand and saved me from the ditch.*

I watched him until I couldn't see him any more. "Let's go, Buddy. Let's go tell the truth."

Buddy and me walked right down the middle of the street. People stood on both sides of the street, talking. Even the men who went into the Valley Tavern every day had left their drinks and come outside. The benches in front of Sue Ann's were full of old guys in bib overalls who chewed and smoked. It was like the day of a parade, or the days when they all wanted to lynch the Walking Man. Most of the talk had something to do with the Baptist church. I couldn't imagine what would be so important down at that church, unless Brother Cross had found that the donation money was stolen. I figured he'd talk the ears off Chief Dinsdale.

Deputy Bob and Cotton were leaning on the fender of Deputy Bob's truck when we got to the jail. Deputy Bob's face was all bruised, like Buddy's and my dad's. Cotton smiled at us. "Look at you two. Golly, Buddy, your face is a mess. And how come you're all wet-lookin', Maggie?"

"Don't be messin' with me, Cotton. I ain't got nothin' more to lose." Buddy raised his fists in a mock fighting position.

"Deputy Bob, I got something important to tell you about Randal," I said.

Before he could say anything, Cotton blurted out, "We know all about Randal."

"How could you? You mean you know he shot at me and that he's the one who killed Angel?"

Deputy Bob got real excited then. He said, "Shot at you? When did this happen? Why?"

Some of the men over at Sue Ann's got up and walked towards us. Deputy Bob put his right arm around my shoulder and his left arm around Buddy's. "You two need to come inside. I have to write this down. The chief is going to want to know all about this." He pushed us toward the door.

"I ain't goin' inside," Buddy said. "I ain't goin' to let my dad get me."

"It'll be all right, Buddy," Deputy Bob said. "He can't get to you—and won't for some time."

"Are you sure?"

"I promise." Deputy Bob stooped down to face Buddy. "There's lots of things the chief and I have to take care of. That business of the whiskey still is one, and him beating on you is another. We got a murder, and now we got something else to deal with." He guided Buddy towards the door. "You'll be okay."

I took Buddy's hand, and he let me hold it. I was kind of surprised, but I held it tight as we went inside. The jail wasn't anything like I thought it would be. There were no bars, and I couldn't even see where Buddy's dad was, so it wasn't scary.

Once inside, Buddy must have felt better too, because he dropped my hand and sat down in a wooden chair in front of the desk. Deputy Bob moved another chair over for me. Then he sat down behind the desk and pulled some paper out of a drawer and wrote something on the top page. Cotton sat on a small bench along the right side of the room, watching us.

Deputy Bob said, "Now, what's this about a shooting?"

"Well," I said, "I had gone into the woods down there by the big willow tree to do some target practice with my BB gun."

"When was this?"

"I don't know for sure. Charlie and me—I mean, Charlie and I came downtown after breakfast and went into Deeter's, so that was probably after nine o'clock. We weren't there too long. Then Charlie went home, and I went down to the woods."

He scribbled on the paper. "Then what?"

"I was in the woods, shooting at pinecones, and suddenly, Randal was there. He had Deeter's stolen gun. I got scared, because I knew it was Deeter's, but I didn't say so."

"What'd he say to you?"

"Not much. He wanted me to shoot the gun, and I didn't want to."

"Then what happened?"

"Well, he shot at some pinecones and knocked them out of the tree. Then he unbuttoned his shirt collar, and that's when I saw Angel's necklace."

Deputy Bob got excited again. "Angel's necklace? How do you know?"

"I've seen it a million times. I know it." I hesitated for a minute. "And I have the cross that was on that necklace." I dug into my jeans, pulled out the cross, and laid it on the table.

"How long have you had this?" He picked it up and turned it over, studying it.

"I found it the day Charlie and me went up to the waterfall. It was on the ground near the path that led up the mountain."

Deputy Bob put the cross on the desk. He spoke soft. "Why didn't you tell us, Maggie?"

"I didn't think it would make any difference. It was something of Angel's, and I had nothing left once I found her. I just wanted to have something of hers."

His brown eyes searched mine. It was hard to look back at him, but I did. I had kept a secret that maybe was important. Now it was out in the open. I knew I would probably lose the cross, but somehow I had always known it wouldn't be mine forever.

"I have to keep this for evidence," he said.

"I know." I watched as he put it in a little yellow envelope.

"Why did he shoot at you?"

"Because when I saw the necklace, I blurted out that I knew it was Angel's, and I accused him of killing Angel and said I would tell Dinsdale."

"How'd you get away?"

"As he started towards me, I shot him in the neck with my BB gun. He dropped the Colt and fell backwards. That's when I ran to the river. I knew he could shoot me, so I jumped in the river and swam underwater towards the other side."

Buddy said, "I heard the shooting. I was over at Mozell's for a couple of nights and stayed with her because I was afraid of going home."

I was stunned. "You stayed at Mozell's?"

Buddy didn't even answer me. He just kept talking to Deputy Bob. "This morning, the Walking Man came there. Wallis helps her, and he can read, and he's nice."

"I know about Wallis, Buddy," the deputy said. "What about the shooting?"

"Well, me and the Walking Man were going towards the highway and heard loud shots. Then we heard Maggie scream. I knew it was Maggie. We ran down the bank to the river. I seen Maggie throw down her gun and jump in. Then Randal came and looked up and down the river, but she was underwater. I guess he couldn't see her. He fired several shots into the Cahaba and then ran back up the bank."

Deputy Bob looked at Cotton. "Go along the river, and find that Daisy. Make some kind of a sign, so we'll know where it was. I don't want somebody else finding it. Hurry, now."

After Cotton left, the deputy turned back to Buddy, "Then what happened?"

"Me and the Walking Man hid in the brush. When Randal was out of sight, we crept closer to the edge of the river and saw Maggie. Wallis grabbed her hand and dragged her out."

Deputy Bob looked at me. "How in the world could you swim that far underwater? That has to be a miracle."

"I've had lots of practice, but I reckon I never swam that far before. I hope I can do it again with Charlie."

"Lord have mercy, Maggie. This has been some week." He eased back in his chair. The bruise on his face looked even worse in the jail's dim light.

From behind a door that led to another room, a voice called, "Deputy Bob. I need to see you."

Buddy whispered, "That's my dad. I know it is."

"You two stay put." Deputy Bob went into the back area. "What d'you need, Alton?"

"I wanna see my boy."

Buddy stiffened. Deputy Bob shut the door. All we could hear were low, muffled voices. We looked around the room, not saying anything. I was trying to hear what was being said, and I think Buddy was doing the same thing. We were as quiet as we could be.

When they stopped talking, Deputy Bob came out and stood in front of Buddy. "Your dad has somethin' to say to you."

"I don't want to see him."

Deputy Bob spoke soft like, "He can't get to you, and as a matter of fact, he doesn't want to. He needs to tell you something. You might be surprised."

Buddy studied the deputy. "Will you leave the door open?"

"I can do that."

Buddy got up real slow and walked to the back room. Deputy Bob stood by the doorway, facing the jail area. I couldn't see Buddy or his dad, but I could hear what they said.

"I know I done wrong by you, Buddy," Alton said.

"You done wrong by your whole family." Buddy sounded like he might cry.

"I know that. I had time to think on it. Your ma needs help. I heard you didn't go home, and I reckon that was my fault."

"You see what you done to my face? You want Ma to see this?"

"Your ma knows I hurt you. I done hurt her too."

Buddy didn't say anything, but his bare feet shuffled on the wooden floor.

"I heard how you saved your friend," Alton said. "That was brave. I'm proud of you."

Buddy's voice got loud. "I ain't proud of you. Tryin' to kill Wallis, and talkin' about niggers and stuff like that. How come you got to be so mean?"

"I don't know. My daddy beat me, and I thought that's how it was done. He didn't care for niggers, but I reckon not all of them's bad."

"You got a ways to go, still talkin' about niggers. Maggie don't like that word, and I don't like it no more. Mozell treated me fine, and washed my face, and tried to ease the pain you caused. You ain't never treated me that good."

"I reckon I ain't. All I can do is try to do better by you, Buddy. You done taught me somethin' 'bout bein' a man. I 'bout made a terrible mistake with Wallis. You saved more'n him by fightin' me. You done saved me. Give me a chance, Buddy."

"I'm gonna have to think on it. I'll go home because of Ma." I heard Buddy's footsteps. Deputy Bob stepped aside as Buddy came back. There were tears in his eyes. I didn't say anything.

The outside door opened, and Cotton came in. He was breathing hard. "I ran all the way. I found it along the bank, near the willow."

"You mark the spot?"

"Sure did, Uncle Bob. I piled rocks there. You can see it easy." Cotton turned to me. "Here's your Daisy. It's kind of dented up from being throwed down."

I turned the Daisy over in my hands and looked at the chip that had been knocked out of the stock. The barrel had several dents. It had taken me a long time to save for this Red Ryder, and I doubted I would ever have a new one again. But I was proud of how it had saved my life.

"It doesn't look too bad to me," I said. "I just hope it shoots straight. I still have to beat Charlie."

Buddy smiled. "Heck, that shot that hit Randal is the best shot of all. Charlie ain't never gonna top that one."

"And he isn't going to beat me at swimming underwater any more, either!"

Buddy laughed. He asked Deputy Bob, "Can we go now?"

"Sure can. I got what I need, but the chief is probably gonna want to talk to you later."

"What'll happen to Randal?" I asked.

"Cotton, you can fill them in on all that happened before they got here. Everybody in town knows it anyway. It ain't no secret." Deputy Bob dug into his pants pocket. "Here's a quarter. Get yourselves some Cokes or RCs and go sit under a tree and be kids. Get outta here."

CHAPTER 25

Cotton, Buddy, and me walked out of the jail just as Deeter came out of his store. He yelled, "What y'all up to? Anytime I see you, I know somethin's going on." He laughed and spit tobacco juice in the gutter.

"We're coming to get some soda pop," Cotton said.

"Who's got the money? Maggie?"

"Heck, no." Cotton said. "I got the money."

"Well, now, that's the third big surprise this mornin'." Deeter opened the screen door and walked inside. We followed.

I know who stole your gun," I said.

"Well, Maggie, I reckon everybody in town knows that." Deeter walked to the ice cooler that held the soda pop. "What'll y'all have?"

"What do you mean, everybody knows? How could they?" I asked.

"I'll have an RC." Cotton said.

Buddy moved closer to the cooler. "How could folks know that? We just done told Deputy Bob."

Deeter popped the top off a bottle of RC and handed it to Cotton. "Where these friends of yours been? In a hole?"

Cotton laughed. "Naw. Maggie's been swimmin', and Buddy was just foolin' around by the river."

"I see. Now, what's y'all's choice?" He looked at Buddy and at me.

"I want a Yoo-hoo," I said.

"Me too." said Buddy.

"Well, I'll tell you what. I'm feelin' good today, because the murder mystery seems solved and we can go back to bein' our safe little town. So I'm goin' to give you children your soda pop and I'll throw in three Moon Pies." Deeter just strung it out all in one breath. I could hardly believe what he was saying. He handed me my Yoo-hoo and Buddy his.

"I still don't understand how anyone could know what happened," I said.

"I'll tell you, soon as we get outside," Cotton said. "While you were at Mozell's, somethin' big happened." Cotton followed Deeter towards the front of the store.

Deeter pulled three Moon Pies off a rack at the front of the store and handed them to us. "Now, y'all run along and play. Be kids." As he smiled at us, a trickle of tobacco juice came out the corner of his mouth. For some reason, I didn't mind seeing it. Deeter was just Deeter.

"Thanks," I said.

"Thank you," Cotton said as he headed out the screen door. "This is some day."

Buddy called back, "I ain't had a Moon Pie in years. Thanks, Deeter."

I heard Deeter walk out the door behind us, and when I looked back, he was watching us go down the street towards the Cahaba. He stood with his hands on his hips until he saw me look back. He waved and then went inside his store.

We were near the movie house and the Valley Tavern before Cotton said anything. "Y'all missed quite a doin' in town. Course, you was involved in quite a doin' yourselves." He took a drink of his RC.

"What's the mystery?" I asked. "How does Deeter know about who stole the gun?" The smell of beer floated out of the tavern as we passed. I bit a chunk out of my Moon Pie.

"It all started with Mrs. Turner this morning."

"I saw her when I was coming out of Deeter's," I said.

"Well, if you had been inside, you would have known she was lookin' to find Randal and to ask Deeter about the gun."

"How come?" Buddy asked.

We had reached the river road. Cotton headed down the path, towards the bench where Ida Mae and I had sat only days before. Me and Buddy followed. Cotton sat on the bench and opened his Moon Pie as he talked. "Mrs. Turner told Deeter she and Randal had got in a bad fight over that gun. She hadn't ever seen it before and asked him where he got it."

"What'd he say?" Buddy asked.

"He wouldn't tell her. That's why she went to see Deeter. When Deeter asked her what the gun looked like and she told him, he knew it was his Colt, and he told her so. Then she really got mad."

"How do you know all this?" I asked.

"'Cause after she left his store, Deeter came over to the jailhouse, and me and Uncle Bob were there. Deeter told my uncle the story. After he left, we waited for the chief to come in, so a report could be made."

"Is that why Dinsdale went speeding up the highway?" I asked.

"Heck, no. That's the third part." Cotton took a big swallow of his RC.

"For Pete's sake," Buddy said. "How many dang parts can there be to stealin' a gun? Seems pretty simple to me."

Cotton laughed. He looked at Buddy. "Well, while you were at Mozell's this morning, and while Maggie was practicin' her shootin', Randal came drivin' through town in his red Crosley."

"But it was purple the other day," I said. "I saw his car when I came out of the woods this morning. But I was so scared, I guess I didn't notice the color."

"Well, it's red now. Anyway, Randal went to work, and he and Deeter got in a heck of a shoutin' match. They came out on the street, hollerin' and fussin'. There were a few folks over by Sue Ann's who heard the whole thing. By the time Uncle Bob and me got outside, Randal had jumped in his car and drove off."

"How come Deputy Bob didn't go after him?" Buddy asked.

"He didn't think it would be such a problem to catch Randal. He said the chief could do that almost anytime, because Randal didn't have anyplace to go and nobody but his mom to take care of him." Cotton popped the last of his Moon Pie into his mouth and licked his fingers.

"He's mighty strange," Buddy offered. "Always has been. Folks say the war made him that way, but I had uncles in the war, and they ain't that strange."

"Strange or not, they need to get him," I said. "He tried to kill me, and he killed Angel."

"That's the third part." Cotton said. "You won't have to worry about Randal anymore."

"Well, I guess I will." I took a swallow of Yoo-hoo.

"Naw, you won't. A couple of hours after Mrs. Turner talked to Deeter, and right after the chief got to the jailhouse, she came back to town. She was yellin' and carryin' on like a rooster in a cockfight. All the folks out on the street heard everthing."

"What got her goin'?" Buddy asked.

"Don't be so secret-like, Cotton," I said. "Get on with it. What's the big deal?"

Cotton looked me square in the eye. "Randal killed himself."

Buddy and I were flabbergasted. I couldn't believe it. "Are you sure?"

"You ain't kiddin', are you, Cotton?" Buddy asked.

"Well, I wouldn't kid about a thing like that. It's true."

"How do you know it's true?" I couldn't believe what Cotton was saying.

"Well, this is gruesome. Are you sure you want to know?"

"Cotton Norwin, don't you fool with me. I can handle anything." I gave him a squinty-eyed look.

"Tell us!" Buddy said. "We done been through awful things already." He ran his hand through his patch of red hair.

"Well, don't say I didn't warn you." Cotton set his empty pop bottle on the bench. "Mrs. Turner went to the church to practice on the organ. That's when she discovered Randal up by the altar."

"What d'you mean?" I asked.

"She told the chief that when she got to the church and saw Randal's car parked in front of the steps, she got scared, because Randal had been actin' crazy, as she put it, for over a week. She knew something was wrong, but she didn't know what, and the theft of the gun made her even more nervous. She was afraid of what he might do."

"What do you mean?" Buddy said.

"She thought he might try to hurt her because of their fight. She said she was almost afraid to go into the church. But then she did, and that's when she saw Randal. This is the gruesome part." He looked intently at us.

"Yeah? What?" I asked.

"She walked right up there, thinking he was sleepin' on the altar steps. And when she got there, she saw the gun first and then realized the whole side of his head had been blown off. Accordin' to her, there was blood and stuff all over the carpet and the wooden pulpit."

"Oh, yuck." I felt sick. "You mean his face was gone?"

"Yep. He must have shot himself right in the head. He left a note, but she didn't read it. She just came straight to the jailhouse."

I couldn't believe any of this. "I want to go home," I said. "I think my mom and dad and Charlie would want me to be there, and that's where I want to be." I picked up my BB gun. "Will you carry the bottle back to Deeter's for me?"

"I'll do it," Buddy said. "You okay, Maggie?"

"I think I am." I really wasn't sure if I was or not. I looked down at the water that flowed under the bridge and saw the mullets swimming in the shadows. The sky was filled with puffy clouds, but I knew it wouldn't rain. It was August. August in Alabama makes summer seem endless, even though fall is only a step away. I smiled at Cotton and Buddy. Then I walked home.

CHAPTER 26

2007

It is August and hot. The Cahaba River runs cool beneath the bridge. I cannot see under the water, so I do not know if mullets still swim there, but I imagine they do. The river does not seem as wide as when I was a kid. But then, most things are smaller than what we remember.

I put the car in gear and drive slowly through town. It is a joy to see the Valley Tavern still there. As I drive by, the aroma of hickory-smoked barbecue wafts out, and I know I will have a sandwich before I leave. The movie house has become a furniture store, but the marquee is still there. It reads: BARGAIN FURNITURE.

I ease the car up to the curb in front of a small café. I know it is Sue Ann's, even though the sign on the window indicates that Betty Joe now runs it. I half expect Wallis Walker to come out, but I know he won't. The year I started college at Florida State, Mom sent a small article about Wallis, and that's when I learned that the Walking Man could indeed, read.

According to the obituary, Wallis Aaron Walker III had been born into a prominent Birmingham family. He had graduated from Alabama Polytechnic Institute, known by locals as Auburn, in the class of 1916 with a degree in astronomy. But like so many young men of that time, he had enlisted in the Army, and by 1917, he had been sent to the front lines in France as a lieutenant in the Army Air Corps. Wallis had received two Purple Hearts for injuries inflicted during the endless air battles, and had come home a changed person.

When I read the obituary, I realized he had lost himself in France. Even though he still talked about stars—and, for a time, had flown below them—he had chosen to wander. For the rest of his life, that's what he had done. I was glad Wallis had wandered into my life, but I remember feeling saddened that I had never really known the man. Maybe that's what being a child is all about.

Before I finished college, Mom and Dad had moved back to Pennsylvania and Charlie had graduated from Alabama with a degree in criminology. He became a law officer in Atlanta, got married and started a family. It was then that I more or less lost touch with Taneytown, except for letters Ida Mae and I had exchanged almost daily.

I open my car door and step out to have a closer look at the town. Deeter's General Store is gone, replaced by a new brick building that houses a Dollar General. I will not go inside. There will never be another Deeter's, and I know that. Perhaps somewhere in the mountains, other general stores come close, but they are not here and never will be again.

As I go up the street toward the jailhouse, a smile creases my face. It is now Norwin's Antiques, and I am delighted. It has to be Cotton's place. The wooden door creaks, and a white-haired man behind the counter stands as I enter. He gives me a puzzled look.

"Maggie. Is it you?"

"Hello, Cotton."

"Well, for Pete's sake. It is you." He comes around the glass case and hugs the bejesus out of me.

"You still are the same ol' Cotton," I say.

"Not quite, but close. My God, what brings you back after all this time?"

"Ida Mae."

"Ida? But she hasn't lived here in over forty years."

"I know. I'll tell you about it, but tell me about yourself first."

He laughs. "Not much to tell. You probably know I was a state trooper for over thirty years. Hard not to follow in Uncle Bob's footsteps."

"I guess not. You always were a little cop, even back then."

"Well, I was working on it, following Wallis and helping Uncle Bob." He smiles. "I got married and raised two kids, a boy and a girl. Tom is a state trooper, and Margaret is a retired school teacher. I'm even a great-grandfather."

"What about your wife?"

"Mary Wilson. You didn't know her, but she was sweet, and she wanted a family life, and so did I. We were happy together, but she died three years ago and that's when I got this place." He pauses. "You want coffee or something?"

"No, Cotton. I'm sorry for your loss."

"It took me a while, but having this store eased the pain and brought back some good memories." He waves his hand. "Look around. I have some things that might interest you."

"You have a lot of stuff in here. Are you going to point things out or leave it a mystery for me to find?"

"I'll direct you a little." He leads me to a glass case on the other side of the room. On the top shelf is a Daisy Red Ryder. "Look familiar?"

I take my glasses out of my pocket for a closer look. "Where in the world did this come from? It's mine. I recognize the dents on the barrel and the chip in the stock."

"I thought you would. I've had it for a long time. Just before your folks moved up north, your dad asked if I would be interested in having it. I guess they didn't think you'd want it anymore." His faded blue eyes twinkle. "You want it now?"

"I'm tempted. But you keep it. For old time's sake. And you can tell your great-grandchildren how it once saved a little girl's life. They won't believe you, but it doesn't matter, does it?"

"No. I know the real story. Come with me, Maggie. I have two other things I want to show you, and maybe you'll want the one."

He walks toward the back room. I realize it must be where the jail cells had been, but only one cell is still intact.

"Now, this is odd," I say, motioning to the cell.

"Actually, I kind of like it. It reminds me of old times and of my whole life's work." He laughs. Then, in a more somber tone, he says, "Look at this." He points to a framed obituary hanging on the outside of the cell.

> *Notice has been received that U.S. Army Sergeant Thomas A. "Buddy" Toliver was killed in action in the Battle of Ia Drang in the central highlands of South Vietnam on November 15, 1965. Mr. Toliver was twenty-five years old and leaves a wife, Betty, née Anderson, and a two-year-old son, Buddy. He is survived by his mother, Ellen, and two younger sisters, Sally Marie and Jane. His father, Alton, was killed in a car wreck in 1959. Memorial services for Sgt. Toliver will be held at the First Baptist Church, Taney-town, on December 20, 1965.*

For a moment, I can see the barefoot, redheaded little boy I had so dearly loved. "Ida told me that he had been killed, but I never saw the notice. It was a long time ago, wasn't it?"

"Sure was. We thought life was all about summers and swimming and shooting pinecones off trees and following the Walking Man. Tough to grow up, huh?"

"At least Buddy got to see more than Taneytown. I wish things could have been different for him, but he must have had a few years of being loved." I look at the obituary once more. "I didn't know his given name was Thomas. Is that why your boy has that name?"

"Thomas is a good name. Same as Margaret." He smiled. "I wanted to remember Buddy. He would have liked that. We were friends, you know." Cotton pushes moisture from his eyes. "Let me show you something else."

He takes my shoulders and turns me toward the back wall. All sorts of odd signs are intermixed with chairs and tables covered with old cameras, books, and records. But one thing stuns me. "Oh, my God, Cotton. A tiger board. A tiger board!"

"I thought you might want that. It came with the place. I don't think they knew what they had."

I pick it up. It's a little faded, but everything is still there: the smiling tiger with all of the strands of steel wire; even the wooden easel is attached to the back. "How much do you want for this?"

"You can have it, Maggie. It wouldn't mean as much to anyone else but you and maybe Charlie. And your folks."

"You don't know, do you?"

"What's that?"

"My parents are gone, Cotton. Dad had a heart attack in 1982, and Mom died the following year from a broken heart. She never got over the loss. It wore her down until finally, she died. The doctor said cardiac arrest, but I knew better."

"I'm so sorry, Maggie. They were great parents. The kind every kid would want. You and Charlie were lucky."

"I know. That's what memory is for. It helps keep people we love alive." I walk to the front of the store, carrying my tiger board.

"You said you came back for Ida Mae. What do you mean?"

"It's a long story, Cotton. But you know most of it already."

He looks at his wristwatch. "You know what? It's time to lock up. Why don't you and I have supper, and you can tell me all about why you came back here? What do you say?"

"Have they still got a bench down by the Cahaba?" I ask.

"Actually, they do. It's a wire mesh thing. Not as pretty as the old wooden one, but it'll do. Why?"

"Why don't you call the Valley Tavern and get us some barbecue sandwiches and some beer to go, and we'll sit by the river. I have something I have to do down there. I'll get my car and be out front in a few minutes."

"That's easy enough. Just like old times."

I step out into the summer heat, walk the short distance to my car, and lay the tiger board on the back seat. I can smell the pine

trees that surround the town. In the distance, a crow caws. I back
out onto Main Street, proceed toward Oak, and turn left. The house
where Angel and Ida Mae lived is still there, but the roses and the
white fence are gone. The Albrights have not lived there for years.
But I have to see it. I also want to see if my house is still there, but I
don't go up the hill on Old Looney Mill. I want to remember my
house like it was so many years ago, and I know it won't be the
same. It can't be.

I drive back and wait in front of the Dollar General. Cotton locks
up his store and yells, "Drive on down to the Valley! I'll walk. They
have our supper ready."

Cotton is still the same, just older. I haven't seen him in over fifty
years, but it's like we've always known each other. I watch him cross
the street and go into the bar, then come out with our food. I drive
over.

"What are you doing?" he asks as he gets in. The smell of barbecue permeates the car.

"Just looking at you.

"What do you see?"

"A friend." Then I point to the sack of food. "And some of the
world's best barbecue."

Cotton notices two boxes on the seat. "What are these?"

"One is Mozell, and one is Ida Mae."

"Now, you will have to explain." Cotton points to an area along
the river's edge. "You can park anywhere here. The bench is down
the bank a little."

I park the car. Cotton carries the sack of food, and I carry the
boxes. As we go down, I am thankful that no one else is there. I
don't want to share this with anyone but my friend. I place the
boxes on the bench. "Let's eat," I say.

"Well, you better explain yourself." He pops the lid on a can of
beer and hands it to me. After a long drink of his beer, he says, "Out
with it. No more mysteries." He picks up the tin box. "Explain."

I laugh. "It was Mozell's. She kept cookies in it, and it was special to her. When I was in college, Mozell died, and Maxine sent it to me, because she said Mozell wanted me to have it." I open the box, revealing store-bought cookies. "You want one?"

"Depends on how old they are," he laughs. "Mozell didn't make these, did she?"

"No, but I wish she had. Hers were a lot better. They were made with love."

He studies the box. "This is an antique for sure, Maggie. I think it might be from the thirties. They had bread boxes like this."

"It is from that time, but don't try to get it from me." I give him my defiant look.

"Still feisty, huh? I won't fight you, Maggie. There must be a story behind this. I know you enough to know that."

"You're right. And some time, I might tell you." I take a long drink of beer and bite a huge hunk out of my sandwich. "Oh, wow. It's just like I remember. Damn, this is good stuff." I watch the water flowing under the bridge. "I wonder what ever happened to Mozell's children, Maxine and Willie. You remember seeing them at Angel's funeral?" I look out to the hills beyond the bridge and see that they have not changed.

"Sure, I remember. I don't know what happened to Willie, but I remember that back when I first started as a state trooper, I saw Maxine at some of the civil-rights rallies in Birmingham and Selma. She was a fireball. Kind of like you." Cotton pokes my arm.

I drink some more of my beer. It is cool. Cotton sits quietly for some time. Then he asks, "So, how did Ida Mae bring you back here? Or is that a mystery that needs to be dragged out of you?"

"It's a long story, Cotton. A lifetime of learning to love who I am and struggling to be accepted."

"I know you. Nothing you tell me will surprise me or change our friendship."

I look him in the eye, and for a moment, I see the Cotton of a faraway time. "Ida Mae and I have been in a loving relationship for over forty years. We traveled the world together and made a home in Florida, near Naples. Sometimes it was hard, but our love for one another got us through. Until about a month ago."

His expression asks the question.

"She died," I answer. "Unexpectedly, with a heart attack."

"Oh, Maggie. I'm so sorry. I know that kind of loss hurts bad."

"At Angel's funeral, I made a promise. That's why I'm here. I promised Angel I would always take care of Ida Mae. As a kid, I had no idea that it would be a lifetime, but I wouldn't change anything." I take his hand in mine. "We can't anyway, can we?"

"No. What is, just is." He pats my hand and squeezes it.

"Anyway, I brought her home. She loved this bench and the bridge. They're not the same, but the river is, and that's where she wanted to be. With the mullets." I pick up the other box. I open it, and the ashes are white and powdery. "Come out onto the bridge," I say.

I go back up the pathway to the road. Cotton follows, with the remains of our supper and Mozell's tin box. We stand on the bridge, looking out over the Cahaba, and I drop the ashes. They float and drift as the slow current takes them away.

"Are you okay, Maggie?"

"I will always be okay," I say. "I have the things that remind me of those I loved." I finger Angel's cross, which was given to Ida Mae and which now dangles from a chain around my neck. I take the green tin box, and we walk back to my car.

"Will I see you again?" he asks.

"I don't know, Cotton. Perhaps." I kiss his cheek. "Thanks for the tiger board. It really is an antique, isn't it?" I laugh. "And to think, I helped make it over fifty years ago. What's that make me?"

"An antique, Maggie. Same as me."

I study his faded blue eyes. "You and me and Charlie. Antiques." I get into my car and start the engine. "Take care of the Daisy, Cotton."

"I will, my friend."

I cross back over the bridge and move onto the highway. I glance into the rearview mirror. For a moment, I think I see Cotton and Buddy, Angel and Ida Mae, and the Walking Man standing on the old iron truss bridge, waving. I smile.

Then I begin the long drive home.

978-0-595-43406-0
0-595-43406-1